The Summer
of the
Bonepile Monster

The Summer
of the
Bonepile Monster

Aileen Kilgore Henderson

Illustrations by Kim Cooper

MILKWEED
EDITIONS

The characters and events in this book are fictitious. Any similarity to real persons, living or dead, is coincidental and not intended by the author.

Published in 1995 by Milkweed Editions
Printed in the United States of America Book design by Will Powers.
The text of this book is set in ITC Bookman.

95 96 97 98 99   5 4 3 2 1

First Edition

Milkweed Editions is a not-for-profit publisher. We gratefully acknowledge support from the Dayton Hudson Foundation for Dayton's and Target Stores; Ecolab Foundation; General Mills Foundation; Honeywell Foundation; Jerome Foundation; John S. and James L. Knight Foundation; The McKnight Foundation; Andrew W. Mellon Foundation; Minnesota State Arts Board through an appropriation by the Minnesota State Legislature; Musser Fund; Challenge and Literature Programs of the National Endowment for the Arts; I. A. O'Shaughnessy Foundation; Piper Jaffray Companies, Inc.; John and Beverly Rollwagen Fund of the Minneapolis Foundation; The St. Paul Companies, Inc.; Star Tribune/Cowles Media Foundation; Surdna Foundation; James R. Thorpe Foundation; Unity Avenue Foundation; Lila Wallace-Reader's Digest Literary Publishers Marketing Development Program, funded through a grant to the Council of Literary Magazines and Presses; and generous individuals.

Library of Congress Cataloging-in-Publication Data
Henderson, Aileen.
    The summer of the bonepile monster / Aileen Henderson.
    illustrator, Kim Cooper.— 1st ed.
        p.   cm.
    Summary: When he and his sister Lou are sent to spend the summer with their blind great-grandmother in the tiny town of Dolliver, Hollis encounters some dark family secrets and vows to uncover them.
    ISBN 1-57131-603-5: $14.95 — ISBN 1-57131-602-7 (pbk) : $6.95
    [1. Mystery and detective stories. 2. Great-grandmothers–Fiction
3. Country life — Fiction. 4. Family problems — Fiction]
I. Cooper, Kim, ill.   II. Title
    PZ7.H37874Su   1994
    [Fic] – dc20   94–33725
                                                                CIP
                                                                 AC

This book is printed on acid-free paper.

To everyone who helped put Hollis's summer
in Dolliver between the covers of a book.

The Summer
of the
Bonepile Monster

1

HOLLIS WATCHED THE DRIVER grasp the handle that whooshed the bus door shut. He saw the driver's eyes reflected in the rearview mirror as he surveyed the passengers dotted about in the seats. Then the motor roared, the inside lights clicked off, and the bus began moving out of the terminal. Hollis pressed his face against the window, staring back to where Mom and Dad, standing apart from each other, were waving. They looked pale and far away in the dirty light.

Sixteen-year-old Lou in the seat beside him was looking back too, leaning across him. The bus slowed, waiting for a chance to turn into the nighttime traffic. Hollis leaped up.

"I'm not going!"

He shoved Lou aside and climbed over her legs to reach the aisle. He forgot there was a step down, and he fell. Lou caught him and held him tight.

"You have to go!" she snarled, not like herself.

Hollis kicked and jerked, trying to free himself. The bus gave a deep growl, then surged out into the traffic lane and picked up speed. Lou was strong from wrestling with tough kids she baby-sat. Hollis couldn't get loose. He felt like exploding. Sweat prickled the edge of his hair as he strained to get away.

9

Then he glimpsed her face in a flash of light from a streetlamp. His sister was crying. The shining tears ran down her cheeks. He felt them warm on his hands. He caught his breath like a pain. He couldn't remember Lou crying ever—Lou, his big sister who always knew what to do when anything went wrong. Lou who could fix whatever broke, who could heal whatever hurt.

"You heard them—we have to go." Her grip on

him loosened and she hugged him in apology, but he could still feel the tears in the dark. He crept slowly back into his seat and curled up, staring out at the city passing by. He heard Lou blow her nose.

"It isn't that they don't want us," she said, sounding more like Lou. "Mom said they've got to have space to try to work things out. And it would be easier if we weren't around."

Hollis thought about how things had been lately at home. He couldn't remember when it started, but his parents seemed to be saying one thing to each other and meaning something else. He had felt they talked in riddles that he couldn't find the answers to. And the riddles weren't happy ones.

Then one day toward the last of school, Mom said, "How would you like to spend the summer in the woods with your dad's grandmother, Grancy? There's a creek you can fish in, and lots of dogs, and—and—." She ran out of words, her lips stretched in a smile that didn't show in her eyes.

"Yes, down at Dolliver," Dad jumped in. "Remember when we used to go there? We had a ball. Fishing, eating watermelons, hunting arrowheads, swimming in the creek." Dad sounded like a car salesman on TV.

"You can be a help to Grancy. She's older now and lost her eyesight, but she's still lots of fun—." Mom floundered.

Dad hurried to fill in the silence. "You can help Fannie-Dove take care of the dogs and cats. You'll like that, won't you? Fannie-Dove is Grancy's helper, and you'll like Fannie-Dove too."

Hollis's head hurt from all the plans his parents

11

made for him and Lou. Their voices sounded so cheerful, like play-acting, and went on and on. He wanted to cover his ears with his hands to keep from hearing.

Now in the dark bus, Hollis watched the city lights trickle away as they hurtled down the road. At the end of that strange road, just after sunrise, they would come to the place where they had to get off the bus. Their suitcases and boxes, stashed in a compartment underneath, contained everything they'd brought for the endless summer in the woods, till Mom and Dad "worked things out."

What if they never worked things out? What if they never sent for them to come home? Maybe his parents would send for Lou and leave him in the woods with these people he didn't remember. Scenes like film clips flitted through his mind:

Mom: "Why haven't you done your homework? You know I can't stand over you every minute."

Dad: "This is the worst report card I ever saw! What's the matter with you?"

And he could hear his own daily refrain: "I hate school! School's no good!"

No, they wouldn't want him to come back. Fright swelled up inside him like an icy snowball growing. He shivered so hard he couldn't breathe. To steady himself, he gripped the arms of the bus seat and tried to see Lou. Her head leaned back and her shoulders drooped. He slipped his hand into hers. She squeezed it and sighed.

The bus went faster and faster toward Dolliver, Alabama, like a humongous vacuum cleaner inhaling the road and leaving nothing but darkness behind.

Out of the silence, Hollis said, "Never-never land, that's where I wish we were going. Never grow up, never change, never—," he struggled to make himself say it, "never divorce, never die."

"That's magic," Lou said. "This is for real."

"Anyway," he whispered, "I hope we never get there."

2

THE BUS DID GET THERE, exactly on time, just past sunrise. The driver dragged their luggage out of the compartment under the bus while Hollis rubbed his eyes and yawned. They were being dumped at what looked like a country store that wasn't even open yet. A rusty old pickup stood nearby, and a wiry old man in overalls was watching them. When the bus pulled away, fuming and growling, the old man came over.

"Be you Lou and Hollis?" he asked. "I'm Mr. Mayhew. Your great-granny sent me for you."

He and Lou loaded their suitcases in the back of the pickup. Hollis couldn't wake up enough to help. He felt like a zombie. Lou opened the truck door and motioned for him to climb in. They squeezed into the truck cab. Hollis had to straddle the gear shift, which came up out of the floor, and every time Mr. Mayhew shifted gears, Hollis had to lurch out of his way.

"It so happened that Fannie-Dove had to go away to visit her daughter," Mr. Mayhew said as his truck struggled up a hill. "But don't worry. My wife'll look in on you and help you get along."

He drove so poky that Hollis had plenty of time to see, but there wasn't much to look at till they came to the top of the hill. Way ahead, the road disappeared into something like a big-doored barn. Hollis stretched his neck to see better. "What's that?"

"Yonder's the covered bridge," Mr. Mayhew said. "We go acrost the creek by way of the covered bridge. Then we're in the woods—my woods, your great-granny's woods, Liam's woods."

Going across the covered bridge was like driving in the front of a house and out the back. The tires made a hollow echo as they rolled over the wooden floor. Below, through a crack in the planks, Hollis glimpsed clear green water flowing along between huge gray rocks. He got the strange feeling of a dream beginning while he was still awake, and Mr. Mayhew's voice sounded far off.

"No nails built this bridge. You can see the wood pegs that hold it together. Made o'heart pine long time ago."

When they came out on the other side, it seemed to Hollis that they had traveled a farther distance than just the span of the creek. There sat a log house and a steepled church beside a cemetery.

"That's where Preacher Henry lives." Mr. Mayhew spoke like a tour guide, pointing out historic attractions. "He's got one o'them tellyfones. And that's his church. My boy's buried in that cemetery, by that big cedar tree." He cleared his throat. "Killed in the war, he was."

Hollis wanted to ask which war, but his mouth wouldn't open. As the truck chugged along, Mr. Mayhew continued, "We'll be to your great-granny's place purty quick now. This road makes a circle and comes back to the bridge. I'll drive you past my house

15

so you can see my chickens. I don't hold with no dogs the way your great-granny does. But chickens are fine, and mine are right handsome. That's my chicken yard there by the strawberry patch. Ain't they purty?"

Proud, shiny chickens with red topknots and curly tails looked through the fence. The pickup bucked down the road past a meadow. A grizzled gray creature, like a bunch of dirty wool, hung his head over the fence, chewing a briar as he watched them pass. He drew back his lips, showing a mouthful of long yellow teeth, and his eyes looked directly at Hollis.

"There's Burdock, the donkey," Mr. Mayhew continued. "He don't belong to anybody, just himself. Next is Liam's place. His great-great-grandpappy helped build the bridge. Liam's got a passel of prize goats, but they're out in his woods this time o'day. And there's the shack where a boy lives with his ma." It was a small, timid-looking house, hiding behind a clump of sunflowers blooming around the door. The boy wasn't in sight.

Farther along the curving road, the truck slowed while Mr. Mayhew fought with the gear shift. Hollis looked to the right where a side road was barred by a gate plastered with signs: "KEEP OUT" "NO TRESPASS-ING" "GIT BACK!" "THIS MEANS YOU!" But what made him sit up straight and his hair stand on end was the big white skull and crossbones on a black board. He stared hard. The skull and bones looked real, not painted.

"Wh-what's that?" he gasped, but Mr. Mayhew speeded up and didn't answer.

Lou was looking back. "That road with all th signs—where does it go?"

"Nowhere." Mr. Mayhew spat out the window. "It's jest a no-count road. Old Bonepile Hollow Road. I didn't mean for you to notice that."

"Piles of bones?" Hollis asked, wishing he had eyes in the back of his head.

Gripping the steering wheel, Mr. Mayhew looked ahead.

"What kind of bones?" Lou insisted.

"Monster bones," Mr. Mayhew growled.

"Monster bones?" Hollis couldn't believe what he heard.

"You mean dinosaurs," guessed Lou.

"Nawwww. Something different. Big as dinosaurs though. Anyway, you don't have any use for that road. You can't go down there."

"Why not?" Hollis demanded.

"Things that go down that road don't ever come back." Mr. Mayhew's voice grew loud and he sounded mad. "That's a wicked place, and don't either of you ever go near it. It's a—a black plague place." The old man's face turned purple and puffed out. He couldn't stop the rush of words. "That place has broke our hearts and cost us dear—all of Dolliver. Don't you for- get—nothing that goes down that road ever comes out." His eyes glassed over with tears. He snapped his jaws shut.

In the sudden silence, Lou and Hollis looked at each other. Around the next curve Mr. Mayhew unclamped his jaws to say, "We're coming to your great-granny's house."

17

Hollis strained his eyes ahead. At first there was nothing but trees; then a dark brown house with a rusty tin roof gradually took shape, like a puzzle being completed. A wire fence, higher than Hollis's head, surrounded it, holding back the woods. Two stout rock chimneys, one on each end of the house, seemed to keep it from falling over. What a place for a ghost-goblin, flashed through Hollis's head. Or a monster! He held his breath, staring. The eerie feeling that had settled over him in the bridge prickled his backbone.

"Your great-granny's place is the oldest in Dolliver, probably built when the bridge was." Mr. Mayhew set down their bags and boxes outside the gate. "I'll not come in, if you two can handle this. Them dogs don't appeal to me." He sprang back in his truck and wobbled away, leaving Hollis and Lou looking through the fence at what must be dozens of leaping, barking dogs with their red tongues hanging out and their white teeth showing.

3

"THEIR TAILS ARE WAGGING," Lou said, peering through the fence at the dogs. "Let's see if they'll let us in."

She lifted the latch, and they dragged their luggage inside the yard. The dogs stopped barking and gathered round, smelling the boxes and suitcases and Hollis and Lou. Now that they weren't leaping about, Hollis could see that there were only five of them, all sizes. When the dogs made up their minds that here were new friends, they began wagging their bodies and grinning a welcome. Hollis and his sister walked slowly toward the porch, which extended the width of the house. Up the steps to the front door they went, escorted by the dogs.

"Grancy?" Lou called.

"Come in, Lou!" a glad voice shouted. The room was cool and dim. At first Hollis couldn't see anybody; then a tiny human being took shape in a big white bed, much the way the house had appeared out of the woods. She had a friendly looking face with a thousand wrinkles, set with shining bright eyes of a mingled color, and her brown twisted hands grasped the white coverlet.

"Is Hollis with you?" The voice from the bed was bigger than the person.

"Yes, Grancy. But why are you in bed?" Lou sounded bewildered.

"It's my summer malady," Grancy explained. "I'll be up and about soon, no doubt."

Hollis stared at her, dumbstruck. What a place! Dad must have meant a different Dolliver from this one: a lean old angry man; a wild donkey that looked like a used dust mop; a real skull and crossbones with threatening signs; one person they were to visit gone away; the other sick in bed with a malady. That word was scary enough, but what about the "black plague" and the unidentified monster bones?

"Can we help you?" Lou asked.

"I'm well fed at the moment, thanks to Molly Mayhew. But you must feed my animals, if you please. I'll tell you how—they are very particular."

So even before they unpacked, Lou and Hollis rolled up their sleeves and began opening cans and bags to feed Grancy's dogs and cats. Grancy was like a royal general, ordering her troops from the big white

20

bed. She ordered the dogs and cats around too. Her eyes were so lively Hollis couldn't believe she was blind. When he was up close to her, he peered into her eyes, so clear and direct looking, but when he held out a pan of dog food and moved it around, Grancy didn't notice.

"I always feel a body can be happier knowing her animals are cared for," Grancy said. "Now you two fix whatever you want for your breakfast. Maybe you'll tell me about your trip while you eat. Lou, can you cook?"

"Yes, Grancy." Lou started for the kitchen.

Hollis felt dizzy and his stomach gnawed from hunger. He was glad when they sat down by Grancy's bed to eat off a small table they'd found folded behind the kitchen door. In all the busyness of the morning, he hadn't one time thought of home. A knot of sadness in his heart reminded him now, but Grancy's quick questions didn't allow him to dwell on it.

Afterwards she said, "Fannie-Dove fixed your rooms before she left. Lou's is next to mine. Hollis, you'll sleep across the hall in the plunder room. That's where everything's stored that's not needed, but too good to throw away—plunder. There's enough space for your bed and a dog or two if you want company."

Hollis had never seen such a room. It was stacked with things—boxes, books, furniture, tools, and toys—he couldn't take it all in. It had one window that reached from floor to ceiling and overlooked the backyard.

"That palm tree's Fannie-Dove's pet," Grancy

called from her bed. "Be careful with it. She says it's happiest by that window."

Later Hollis told Grancy, "My room is weird."

She laughed. "It sort of sums up your ancestors who've lived in this house since they came here long ago. You can look at whatever you want to—just be careful that nothing falls on you."

Hollis took a deep breath and stepped closer. "What I really want to know—what Mr. Mayhew wouldn't tell me—is about those monster bones on that road."

Grancy's face looked blank with surprise. After a pause she said, "There are many big bones in the hollow that road leads to, very old bones."

"Whose bones?"

"Antediluvian monster bones." Grancy said every syllable exactly. "IMMENSE antediluvian monster bones."

Hollis wasn't sure what this meant, but there was something else he wanted to know first. "Why is Mr. Mayhew mad about the immense antediluvian monster bones? Whose skull is that nailed up by the gate?"

Grancy lay quiet for a minute. "We'll have to talk about that another day," she finally said. "Wouldn't you like to go outside and get to know my dogs?"

Hollis wanted to know about the monsters. But he didn't dare ask again for fear she might never tell him. He tucked her promise into a pocket of his mind and went outside to sit on the porch steps. The dogs crowded around him, smiling and wagging. Home-sickness overwhelmed him like a steamroller that wouldn't stop, that rolled right over him, flattening him into the ground. This place was too quiet, with the woods crowding right up against the fence. Back home at their apartment he could always hear sirens and whistles and car horns. In this silence he felt deaf. And there was nothing to see. Anytime, day or night, when he looked out their fifteenth-floor window he could see lights, people, cars, fire engines.

Back there I'd be watching a movie, or TV, or maybe calling up one of my friends, he thought. Why, he hadn't seen a television anywhere in Grancy's house. Nor heard a telephone ring.

The biggest dog, shaggy with feathery leg plumes, crowded close against him and laid his head on Hollis's shoulder. Hollis put his arms around the dog and leaned on him, letting some of the dog's furry gladness seep into the sad emptiness inside his chest.

Mrs. Mayhew came walking out of the woods in late afternoon. She looked just like Mr. Mayhew except cleaner, and she wore a dress and an apron instead of overalls. The three of them did the chores with Grancy calling out orders from her bed. When the animals had been fed and supper made ready, Mrs. Mayhew started home.

"I don't mind coming over here a bit," she told Grancy as she fitted a bonnet over her hair. "But it seems to me you got two mighty good helpers here, and maybe you don't need me."

Grancy agreed.

Hollis, standing at the foot of the bed, couldn't help grinning. Lou looked tired, but happier than she had in a long time.

They walked with Mrs. Mayhew to the gate. As it closed behind her, she said, "Now snap the lock shut. Everybody in Dolliver locks their yard at night." Before they could question her, she trotted down the hill and vanished into the forest. Her path must pass near to Bonepile Hollow, Hollis thought. He promised himself that he would take that way one day soon and see what he could see. But for now he had all he could handle right here.

He rattled the gate to make certain it was secure. That seemed to signal the trees outside the fence to shake their thick leaves like angry horses tossing their manes. A chill, moist wind swirled around them. The dogs stood with their ears at attention, listening, watching.

"What was that?" Lou whispered.

"Nothing," Hollis managed to say, but all of them scurried toward the safety of the house.

4

THAT FIRST NIGHT Hollis dreaded going into his room.
For one thing, it had no light. Grancy furnished him
with a big flashlight that he tested as soon as he shut
the plunder-room door. He swung it around like
a spotlight, examining his bed, the old books and
magazines stacked on shelves, the toys and junk.
Fannie-Dove's palm tree looked black and cast an
even blacker shadow on the open window behind it.
He snapped off the light.

He was so tired his teeth ached. Grancy had
kept him and Lou hopping all day. Every time they
sounded homesick or worried, Hollis noticed, she assigned them two or three more jobs to do. From her
command post in the big white bed, her voice boomed
out like an air-traffic controller up in the tower ordering planes to do this and to go there. He couldn't wait
to stretch out and sleep.

He backed up and took a running jump into the
bed the way he did at home, expecting to bounce.
Instead, he sank in the soft feather mattress and lay
there like a big stone. As he turned on his side, he
could hear feathers crunching and could smell a
clean feathery odor that tickled his nose and made
him want to sneeze. He pulled the long weiner-
shaped pillow Grancy called a bolster under his head,

and he thought back over the day. He thought about the odd feeling he got rumbling through the covered bridge, like a cold hand reaching inside his chest and squeezing his heart. He thought of Mr. Mayhew and the monster bones nobody would talk about and the white skull with empty eye sockets. He thought of Grancy, so chipper and bright, yet sightless and sick with a "summer malady."

One thing he would not think of was Mom and Dad at the bus station last night. He tossed about and kicked the covers. What time was it? He stared toward the window, a lighter rectangle in the blackness of the room. It made a frame for Fannie-Dove's palm, silhouetted against the outside night. Sleep wouldn't come, though he was ready.

He pulled himself out of the depths of the feather bed and tiptoed to the window. Not a sound out there, but he could see the hulking blackness of the woods that stood between Grancy's house and Bonepile Hollow. Above the silent woods the big stars hung, pulsing with bright color. Suddenly a horrible wrenching noise split the night air. It was a great exhalation of racket and then a violent seesawing back and forth that went on and on while Hollis stood riveted to the window. It came from somewhere within the woods and seemed to Hollis to be a fitting cry for an antediluvian monster. He took another flying leap into his bed, knowing this time that he would sink, and glad of it. He heard the whirring of Grancy's mantel clock, then the booming of the hour. He began counting but fell asleep before the clock finished.

Next day at breakfast he said, "I heard an ante-diluvian monster last night."

Grancy's wrinkled face tightened with puzzlement. "What did it sound like?"

Hollis stood tall, took a deep breath, and imitated what he'd heard. It sounded awful. The cats hid under the bed and Lou covered her ears.

Grancy laughed and clapped her hands. "Splendid! You did it just right. That's Burdock."

"The donkey?" Hollis doubted that any known animal could sound like that.

"Burdock likes to wake up everybody, so he brays a lot at night." Grancy sounded relieved that she could explain the mystery. "You must take my word for it, Hollis. It's the donkey. Don't you be going out after dark to investigate any noise. We'll be safe here with the gate locked and the dogs on guard. Don't ever let the dogs out of the yard either."

She looked so serious Hollis asked, "Why?"

Grancy hesitated. "It's just better if they stay at home, and you too." She wouldn't say anymore, but Hollis found out more late in the afternoon when Mrs. Mayhew came to see how they were getting along. When she was leaving Hollis walked through the gate with her.

"Where does this path go?"

"Down this hill past Fannie-Dove's peanut patch, up the other hill, and across the loop road to my house," she said, swinging along.

"I'll come with you," Hollis said.

"Oh, no!" she exclaimed, stopping in midstep. "You can't do that!"

"Why not?" he asked. "I want to see what's down there."

"Didn't anybody tell you? Don't you know?" Mrs. Mayhew sputtered. "You can't go wandering around in these woods by yourself."

"But you do." Hollis was careful to speak politely. "Why can't I?"

"You're—you're an Orr," she said, her eyes big. "Orrs can't—aren't safe in the woods."

"Why? Will an antediluvian monster get me?"

"Law! Have mercy! Don't talk about that." She glanced around as if she thought something was listening. "You go back inside the fence. Hurry. Lock up." And she strode off into the trees.

Hollis watched her go, afraid, yet wanting to know. The sun was setting, the shadows were long, but still daylight was everywhere. What could hurt him? Why was she, a Mayhew, safe, and he, an Orr, in danger? His mind busily organized the new clues he had provoked from Mrs. Mayhew.

"Hollis!" Lou called from the window. "Grancy says come back in the yard."

He slowly retraced his steps to the house. All the dogs were watching and listening. Even they looked anxious. What did they know? Was that awful sound he heard at night really the donkey braying or was Grancy covering up?

5

THE SECOND NIGHT Hollis spent in the plunder room transformed the Dolliver summer for him. Everything seemed the same to begin with, and he was just as tired as the night before. He stood again at the window, watching the outside take shape in the night—the backyard, then the protective fence, beyond that the peanut patch, then the ominous dark bulk of trees rearing their crowns out of Bonepile Hollow, dangling with vines that whispered and swayed. And somewhere beyond them the powerful, ragged explosions of sound that Grancy called Burdock the donkey. Doubt still fretted Hollis's mind about that. Donkeys said, "Hee haw, hee haw," he thought. What he had heard was nothing like "Hee haw, hee haw." He shuddered, remembering.

As he turned from the window, his shoulder brushed Fannie-Dove's palm. He had watered it today, at Grancy's urging. "Palms like to keep wet feet," she said and ordered him to water the other pet plants too, even the vine at the mailbox. No letter from home today. He forced himself not to think about what might be going on there. He willed himself to go to sleep.

Now Grancy's mantel clock whirred and struck eleven. He heard dog footsteps swishing through grass past his window—the five on patrol. He wondered if Lou and Grancy were sleeping. No sound now. Wasn't there a saying about midnight magic? Maybe here in the plunder room of this old house in the Dolliver woods, midnight might be the witching hour. With his thoughts focused on the halfway point till morning, a quietness came over him. He heard a faint rustling near the bed, but he was fading far away. The rustling came again. Then he realized he could hear music, a voice singing, like a radio. He listened as in a dream. The sound grew louder, a happy song trilling like a bird. But he knew there wasn't a radio or bird here. He had checked the room carefully in daylight.

Struggling upright in the feather bed, he listened. It *is* a song, he thought. Here in this room. A melody of "Ha ha ha ha ha ha" over and over. It came from near the palm tree, rising and falling tunefully, flowing on and on. Hollis pushed back the quilt and got out of bed with great care. Clutching the flashlight he crept barefoot across the floor toward the window. The laughing song grew louder. Hollis's heart beat so hard he trembled. Now he could almost touch the palm. He aimed the flashlight at the sound and pressed the button. No! He couldn't believe what he saw in the circle of light. Beneath the palm tree in the redwood planter stood a mouse! On its hind legs! With its head up! Hollis saw its throat throbbing and the pointed nose vibrating as the mouse warbled, "Ha ha ha ha ha ha." It looked like a tiny potbellied man in a neat fur suit singing a part in an opera.

Hollis stared hard at the mouse as it sang on and

on. Is this a dream? he wondered. He gave himself a sharp pinch. Ouch! He was awake for sure, and the mouse was still singing. It paid no attention to the light nor to Hollis. He could see its bright black eyes, small rounded ears, soft gray fur coat with the tail curving tidily round its feet. How proud and happy it looked. Hollis felt as if he were seeing the first mouse in the whole world, as if the mouse had just been created.

He must have stood there for fifteen minutes, watching and listening. At the end of the concert, the mouse lowered its front paws and sat still for a moment, then vanished in an eye blink.

Dazed, Hollis made his way back to bed, but then he remembered Grancy's cats. Where did they sleep?

31

Could they get inside this room? He checked the hall door to make sure it was shut tight before hopping back under the covers. He lay there thinking. Nobody would believe what had happened. He wouldn't believe it himself except for that pinch. A laughing mouse! A singing mouse! Here in his room! Tomorrow I'll bring it food, he planned. And I've got to keep the door shut. Mustn't let a cat catch it. But I won't tell anybody, not yet. Not even Lou. He hugged his secret to him.

Grancy's clock whirred and began striking. Hollis grinned. This is midnight, he thought, and look what's happened. Since coming through the covered bridge to Dolliver, he had felt as if he'd fallen through a crack in time, into the long ago where people talked and acted around a terrifying mystery they all pretended wasn't there. But now, added to that, he had the midnight magic of tonight. Hollis fell asleep smiling.

The next thing he heard was Lou pounding on his door. "Grancy says to stir your stump. She's ready for breakfast."

"Coming," he yawned, pulling on his clothes. What a short night. Then he remembered the mouse. Fannie-Dove's pet palm looked the same as yesterday. Nothing stirred around its base in the redwood planter. Something was sure stirring there last night! Was it true? It had to be. He felt yet the sting of that pinch on his arm. He had been awake, and it really happened. He felt light and—yes—happy as he made sure the plunder-room door shut behind him.

The kitchen smelled so good his mouth watered. First thing he had to arrange Grancy's tray and carry it to her bed without spilling the coffee from her big mug.

"Yum, yum." Grancy smacked her lips when she heard him coming.

Hollis thought about what he'd need to know if he couldn't see, so he'd understand how to help Grancy.

"Here's your tray," he explained, setting it across her lap. "Your plate's in the middle, with pancakes and bacon. Your fork and napkin are to the left of your plate, the coffee's hot and at two o'clock. Your orange juice is at eleven o'clock." Grancy touched each thing as Hollis located it, then she settled into eating.

"Tasty pancakes," she pronounced. "How many did you bring me?"

"Three," said Hollis, watching how neatly she carried the food to her mouth.

"I'll need three more," she said, "and another bacon. I'm partial to blackberry syrup too."

Hollis trotted back to the kitchen, where Lou helped him with the reorder.

"I eat like a field hand," Grancy said, pleased with herself. "You're a good cook, Lou. You take after me."

Hollis ate like a field hand too, and he couldn't keep from smiling. Lou watched him suspiciously. "What's happened to you? Yesterday you hated coming here."

He was bursting to tell her and Grancy about the laughing mouse, but what if it was another of Grancy's secrets, like Bonepile Hollow? Better keep quiet. Instead of answering he stacked their empty plates on Grancy's tray and took them to the kitchen.

33

From that point on, the day shot off like a rocket. Just as she had the first day, Grancy kept them busy, one job after the other. Hollis pitched into the kitchen cleanup with such good cheer that Lou's eyebrows raised in wonder. He protested that he LIKED to get his hands in dishwater and do the other kitchen chores, when what he had in mind was to sneak some tidbits for his mouse.

By the time the morning jobs were finished and Grancy taken care of, the mailman came in his dusty black pickup. Today, however, he rolled right past Grancy's mailbox standing there by the side of the road with Fannie-Dove's lacy green vine clambering up the post and frothing red blossoms over the top.

"No letter from home," Lou said, looking out the window. Hollis felt disappointed too.

"Too soon," Grancy assured them. "You'll be hearing." After lunch, while Lou read aloud to Grancy, Hollis hurried to his room, his pockets bulging with mouse food. He had some reading of his own to do as soon as he arranged the cheese and biscuits under Fannie-Dove's palm. He intended to rummage in some old natural history books he had seen on the shelves. Maybe there would be information about mice in them.

Before long he found the topic "Musical Mice," which told about ordinary people like Hollis who had seen and heard singing mice and also about scientists who had observed them. Among the names was one that Hollis recognized as very famous, Charles Darwin. One man had even written down the notes of his mouse's songs. A girl who played the piano every evening told how a mouse appeared as soon as she struck the first note, and sang along with her tunes, night after night. Musical mice, the book noted, were attracted to radio music too.

One person claimed the mouse he heard sounded like a bell, another said a flute, yet another a bird. Then there was the man who found a mouse sitting in a shoe filled with popcorn in a closet. He declared it sang exactly like his canary. But Hollis remembered his mouse's song as more like a singing laugh. He slipped the books back on the shelf. "My mouse is real, truly real," he exulted. He decided he would study his mouse as these writers had and keep a detailed record of everything he observed about it.

On the shelves, he found an old school tablet and a bunch of pencils, just what he needed for his journal. Why not begin now? By the time for evening chores, Hollis had covered several pages and worn all the pencils down.

6

AT SUPPER he hid a chunk of peanut butter in a paper towel and smuggled it to his room. What a feast—too much for any one mouse, he knew. But suppose it didn't like biscuits? Or cheese? Or peanut butter? Now the mouse had a choice of menu. And suppose it brought along some relatives tonight? Popcorn! That's what he needed.

Going into Grancy's room, he found her teaching Lou how to make a lacy something called tatting. Lou sat on the bed while Grancy showed her how to hold the "shuttle", a small, polished piece of bone pointed on both ends. Lou's face twisted with concentration. One cat batted around the ball of thread. The other cat lay curled up on the coverlet. An electric lamp hung from the ceiling as it did in all the rooms except the plunder room. Hollis didn't care that his room had no light. He had a songful mouse!

"Grancy, do you have any popcorn?" he asked, edging up to the bed.

"No, I've not had popcorn since I quit farming," Grancy said, feeling to make sure the thin line of thread was circled accurately around Lou's left hand.

Hollis paused, marveling that Grancy seemed to have eyes in the tips of her fingers. Then he said loudly, "I wish we had popcorn."

"Add it to the list in the kitchen," Grancy said. "At the end of the week, Preacher Henry takes our list to the store and brings us what we need."

Hollis wrote "popcorn" in big letters so Preacher Henry would be sure to see it. Then he collected the pencils and sharpened them with a small kitchen knife. After that he told the others good night and went to the plunder room, making sure he latched the door. He lay quivering with expectation, his ears tuned toward the palm tree. What a long time it took for Lou and Grancy to quiet down. He heard the dogs walk around the yard past his window on patrol, then the clock struck ten and there was silence.

Every so often he raised himself up in the feather bed, to make sure he stayed awake. The mouse might not come back again, but those he had read about usually did. He wouldn't give up hope. After the clock struck eleven, he decided to sit on a low bench near the palm, holding tight to the flashlight, to make sure he didn't miss the songster.

He listened. A swish. A rustle. At last! He didn't hesitate to switch on the flashlight because the book had assured him singing mice did not fear a light. Sure enough, there was the mouse, gnawing first on the biscuit, then the cheese, and tasting the peanut butter. Hollis watched as it sat up, daintily holding a large crumb in its paws and rapidly chewing. When it had enough, like a tiny cat it groomed itself, especially its whiskers and face. Then, wonder of wonders, it threw out its white chest, held up its head, and sang! Hollis forgot all time. He forgot where he was. He forgot who he was.

Just past the midnight striking of the clock, the mouse dropped to all fours, ran its lips over what was left of the food, then vanished in thin air as it had the night before. Hollis's hand, holding the flashlight for so long, had stiffened, and his feet tingled. He crawled between the covers, impressing on his mind every detail of what he had seen and heard. Tomorrow he would write it all down in his continuing "Journal of the Musical Mouse."

He always hopped out of bed early, even when he'd stayed up late waiting for the mouse. Immediately, he looked out his window, beyond the back fence, over Fannie-Dove's peanut patch, to the solid wall of green that shielded Bonepile Hollow. Nothing ever seemed to change there, no sound ever disrupted the silence except at night what Grancy called Burdock. But Hollis did not forget that something sinister hid in the Hollow.

So far he knew only what he had gleaned from Mr. Mayhew (anger, monster bones, what goes down there doesn't come back); what Grancy had said (antediluvian monster bones, talk about it another day); and Mrs. Mayhew (Orrs are not safe here). Nobody explained anything. Or if they did, Hollis couldn't believe them, like Burdock braying. The harder it was to get answers to his questions, the more determined he became to find a way. He would bide his time, looking and listening.

The days went by so fast Hollis felt that somebody had punched the fast forward button and forgot to let go. Once the day cranked up and took off, he didn't have a minute to ponder and speculate about his mouse and the Hollow. As soon as breakfast was over, he and Lou set to work, ticking off jobs on an invisible list, every day the same. Hollis thought of the jobs in capital letters:

FEED THE TWO CATS. Thompkins and Samantha ate on the kitchen table among pots of Fannie-Dove's plants. Each cat had its own bowl and wouldn't eat out of any other. They refused to eat out of dirty bowls too, as Hollis discovered one day when he forgot to wash the cat dishes. The cats weren't interested in him as a boy; to them he was just a pair of hands that dished out their menu. Hollis didn't care. He wasn't much interested in them either. Samantha was nothing but a blotch of colors, kind of messy looking, as if some little kid had smeared her with finger paints. Even worse, her eyes didn't match—one was blue and one was yellow. Thompkins was rounded and striped. He looked like a walking watermelon, only gray instead of green. Hollis thought him a little slow-witted.

FEED THE FIVE DOGS in the front yard. Each one had its own bowl too and wouldn't eat out of anybody else's. Right away, Hollis and the dogs became chums. Maudie's legs didn't always work right, but Hollis was careful to look away when she was having trouble so she wouldn't be embarrassed. "It's because she's so old," Grancy told him. "I've had her the longest of all my dogs." Shitepoke had tall skinny legs holding up a tiny body. "Like that swamp bird," Grancy explained. "He looks like a shitepoke." Ring was all brown except for a neat white circle around his neck like a shirt collar. Blackie resembled a sharp-nosed dark fox. From the first, Hollis's favorite had been big King David with the feathery leg plumes. He looked at Hollis with such glad brown eyes and seemed always to understand how Hollis felt.

FEED THE WILD BIRDS. Hollis learned to shinny up a pole to fill bird feeders hung along arms like branches. He memorized what seeds went in which feeders: sunflower for cardinals, niger for goldfinches, peanuts for tufted titmice, cracked corn for jays, millet for wrens. "Don't overlook any of the seeds," Grancy warned, "else the birds that like that kind will sit around the house all day fussing. And be sure to fill the bird bath."

WASH DISHES AND CLEAN UP THE KITCHEN, COL-LECT ALL ANIMAL DISHES (Hollis counted them to make sure—seven), dunk them in sudsy water, and set them in the sun to dry.

SWEEP THE REST OF THE HOUSE, INCLUDING THE FRONT PORCH, but not the plunder room. "Don't go in my room." Hollis sounded like Grancy giving orders. "Keep the door shut, and no cats allowed."

HELP GRANCY INTO HER BIG CHAIR TO DRINK HER APPLE JUICE. They did this at midmorning. She was easy to help because she was so small. "I don't weigh much more than a puffball," she'd say.

BRUSH GRANCY'S LONG WHITE HAIR. Hollis did this while Lou read aloud from one of the comic books he'd brought from home. They laughed a lot, especially over the way Lou changed her voice to fit the comic characters. Sometimes she got mixed up and used the wrong voice. Hollis liked brushing Grancy's hair. It was fine and smooth as corn silk. Her skin

40

was nice to touch too—dry, but soft and cool, like the talc rock in his collection at home. After Hollis combed the tangles out of Grancy's hair, he braided it according to her directions, bringing the three strands of the braid together at the end with a rubber band. Grancy looked neat and refreshed, sitting there with Lou and Hollis taking care of her. While all this was going on, the dogs came on the porch, their toenails clickety-clacking across the floorboards, and spied in the windows, hoping to be invited inside for a rumpus.

OPEN THE FRONT DOOR. The dogs exploded into the room, gathering around Grancy, each one waiting a turn for Grancy's petting and praising. She bragged on them for every little thing she could think of and never repeated herself. Occasionally a dog became so proud it decided to keep Grancy all its own. Then a big fight erupted—snarling, shouldering, teeth-snapping—and dog fur flew every which way on the clean floor. Hollis noticed the dogs were careful not to jostle Grancy during these squabbles. It was as if they knew she was frail and needed to be cared for. Dignified Maudie never took part in such a fracas. Samantha and Thompkins, perched on Grancy's chair back, kept aloof too, but they wanted their share of attention.

GO TO THE MAILBOX FOR THE MAIL, TAKING A PAIL OF WATER FOR FANNIE-DOVE'S VINE. If Hollis and Lou had written home, or if Grancy had dictated to them a postcard for Fannie-Dove, they raised the red flag on the box to tell the mailman to stop. If the red flag was down, he stopped only if he had a letter for

41

them. Then they raced to the box, forgetting the pail of water in their haste for some word from home.

On the day they found a letter from Mom in the box, Hollis and Lou got into a big fight. Grancy said later that she thought it was the dogs going at each other tooth-and-nail again. Hollis wanted to be first to open the letter; Lou thought she should be. They ended up back in Grancy's room, with her holding the crumpled letter, which had been nearly snatched in two between them. "I know you're both anxious to hear how things are working out," she said in the soft voice she used with angry dogs. "I am too. But none of us will know if you shred the letter."

Hollis knew she was right, and he knew also that Lou could read Mom's handwriting easier than he could. He lay back across the foot of Grancy's bed, his chest still heaving from their struggle, while Lou opened the envelope. The nubs decorating Grancy's white bedspread indented his back as he concentrated on the meaning of the words Lou read.

Afterwards the three of them discussed the letter.

Even though Mom wrote about ordinary happenings and mentioned Dad only to say they were both going once a week to talk with a counselor, Hollis felt a strange hope. Instead of Grancy, Lou, and Hollis each carrying the unhappiness of his parents' estrangement alone, now they helped each other carry it. Never at home had anyone spoken aloud of the trouble that they all knew was there, clouding their lives. But here in this old room, which Hollis felt sure had contained much grief and happiness, he began to feel a certain peace. Now their sorrow was out in the open, he could see that it wasn't his fault after all, which made it somehow less terrible.

LUNCH. Both Hollis and Lou made and served lunch, then cleaned the kitchen.

READ THE NEWSPAPER TO GRANCY. Lou did this, while Hollis slipped into the plunder room to search for more mouse information in the old books and to write in his journal. Some nights the mouse didn't show, but Hollis always had something to write. Then one day, when he hadn't seen the mouse for a while, he began drawing pictures to illustrate his notes —this made him feel as if the mouse were right there with him because he had to re-create his memories in every detail. The tablet was filling up fast with writings and drawings on both sides of the pages.

FEED THE ANIMALS AGAIN, LOCK THE GATE, AND MAKE SUPPER came next on the list. Then after supper Lou and Hollis sometimes wrote home. Grancy suggested they shouldn't mention that Fannie-Dove was away. "We're getting along so well," she said. "And they have enough to worry about." When Grancy took a notion, she'd dictate a postcard for Fannie-Dove, telling her to be sure and send word before she came back. Other times, Lou tatted, her shuttle flying and her lace growing longer, while Hollis and Grancy stumped each other with made-up riddles.

Then about nine-thirty, they tucked Grancy in and put out her light. Thompkins and Samantha were already asleep on the bed. The dogs snored on the porch. Each night when Hollis shut the plunder-room door, he felt content if he had checked everything off his imaginary list of chores. He would close the day by updating his "Journal of the Musical Mouse." By now he knew he had to think of a different title because what he wrote in the tablet was not only about his mouse. It was about a mystery that grew bigger as time passed, that overshadowed every day in Dolliver, a mystery that nobody would help Hollis solve.

IN THE MORNINGS when he took the big key off the hook by the fireplace and went out to unlock the yard gate, Hollis pondered why everyone in Dolliver locked their yard gates at night. Why was it all right for gates to be unlocked during the day, but as soon as dark began closing in, they had to be locked? When he asked Grancy, she said, "Because it's better that way." Hollis thought that an unsatisfactory answer, but watching her fingers nervously pulling at the nubs on her bedspread, he knew he shouldn't ask any more questions.

Another big key hung on the hook by the fireplace. Hollis used it each Sunday night to wind the clock that squatted in the middle of the mantelpiece. Whenever he took down either key, he glanced at the big painting hanging above the clock. The man in the painting looked right back at Hollis with a merry glint in his deep blue eyes. He looked as if he'd just thought of a prank to play on Hollis but didn't want him to suspect anything. Between those two mischievous eyes, his nose arched out boldly, and below was a straight, firm mouth enclosed on either end with deep wrinkles, like parentheses, set in a strong chin.

"Your great-grandpa," Grancy said when Hollis asked. "My husband. Will Orr himself. I painted him

45

from memory, after he was dead and buried." She paused, thinking. "Painting him brought him back to me in a way and made my hurting bearable." Hollis thought of how drawing his mouse made him feel closer to it, as if he hadn't lost it after all. He understood how Grancy felt.

"Did you ever see such larky eyes?" Grancy asked. "Orr men have those indigo blue eyes. Deep violet-blue, like the blue in the rainbow. Your grandfather had them, and your father." Yes, the eyes were like Dad's, except Dad hadn't looked that merry in a long time. "You, too, Hollis, have the Orr eyes. I well remember how you looked when I could see and your parents brought you here."

Hollis hadn't thought much about his eyes. Orr eyes, like his ancestors, "indigo blue," the blue of the rainbow! He puffed out his chest. But suddenly Grancy was saying in a forlorn voice, "Oh, Will, how I wish you hadn't gone down there that day. You said you'd be all right, but you didn't come back." Her face crumpled, and Hollis knew she had forgotten he was there. "Those bones—those awful bones!" Grancy shuddered and sopped her tears with a corner of the bedspread.

After a while, she cleared her throat, adjusted her face and said, "With his own hands he built that clock out of a cherry tree from our woods. Every Sunday night he'd take that key and wind it, just the way you do, Hollis."

"Who's this girl in the small picture?" Lou asked, dusting the mantel.

Grancy didn't answer right away.

"She's smiling and kinda out of focus," Hollis said, curious too.

"That's my girl, Josie," Grancy said in a low voice. "She lived here once, but now she's gone away to Memphis." She looked so sorrowful Hollis wanted to put his arms around her. He opened his mouth to ask why, but Lou frowned a "no" at him.

After that Hollis was more mystified than ever. Grancy had said that Grandpa Will had "gone down there" and "he didn't come back." Those words echoed what Mr. Mayhew had said: "Things that go down that road don't ever come back." He was sure there had to be a connection between Grandpa Will's death and Bonepile Hollow; between Grancy's fear and grief, and Bonepile Hollow. In his journal he sifted out of the day-to-day chores whatever clues he picked up to the mystery. Someday, he knew, they would all fit together.

The cherry-wood clock struck eleven. Hollis closed the tablet and switched off the flashlight, which was growing so dim he could hardly see his penciled words on the paper. Tomorrow he must add "flashlight battery" to Preacher Henry's shopping list in the kitchen. But for tonight, no mouse, no solution to the secret of the Hollow. He vowed not to give up on either one.

Grancy kept them busy with the same chores every day, but once in a while she sprang a surprise, like the morning she proclaimed, "I hereby appoint you kudzu exterminator, Hollis. Every summer, that ol' kudzu vine sneaks out of Bonepile Hollow and tries to

47

claim Fannie-Dove's peanut patch. Fannie-Dove has to fight it like a savage. She's not here, so you, Hollis, must save the peanut patch."

Hollis didn't feel like saving anything, especially not a peanut patch. "I don't know how," he muttered.

"You have to arm yourself," she said. "Put on my gloves—they'll fit you just right. Wear your knee boots. Take a hedge clipper, a chop-ax, the froe, a hoe, and the mattock. Fannie-Dove keeps them in the wheelbarrow under the log shed." Grancy described the tools so he'd know what he was using. She ended with, "And remember—don't stand still more than five minutes, else the kudzu will cover you too."

Hollis thought Grancy must be joking, but he wasn't so sure when he rolled the wheelbarrow loaded with his weapons into the peanut patch. It lay between Bonepile Hollow and Mrs. Mayhew's path home. Nervously, he glanced back at the house. He could see his window with the palm tree peeking out. He didn't feel so brave now that he was out here alone on the rim of the Hollow. Grancy wouldn't have sent him here if there was danger, he told himself.

He looked toward Bonepile Hollow, the source of the kudzu. The vine had covered everything that stood in its way as it inched out of the Hollow and up the hill toward the peanut patch and Grancy's house. He could see, under the thick blanket of green, the outline of tall trees and the roof peak of some building the vine had blotted out. Hollis stared at the sea of green, realizing that kudzu was another kind of monster. If it were not stopped here, it would move on over the fence, over Grancy's house, over the road. Even now its fuzzy tendrils reached out toward his legs, twining around his ankles, trying to bind him and cover him. Kudzu could make him into a green statue, standing in the middle of an ex-peanut patch. He shivered.

"Don't stand still more than five minutes," Grancy had warned.

Hollis set to work, chopping, stomping, pulling. The vines were like rubber—they stretched and stretched and refused to break. The clippers chewed at them but couldn't cut through their tough fibers. The pick was better. He dug up several stringy roots, but mostly he had to chop the vines off at ground level. The sharp blade of the chop-ax slashed right and left, but the mattock, which he could use for chopping or digging, was best of all. The froe he found to be heavy and dull. He laid it back in the wheelbarrow, wondering how Fannie-Dove could use it for anything.

Whenever he had uprooted a pile of vines, he dragged them to a bare spot and spread them out to die in the hot sun. "Don't leave them in the patch," Grancy had told him. "They'll put down roots and start crawling again."

Working, sweating, groaning, Hollis could see he was making headway, driving the enemy back to its lair in Bonepile Hollow. Every so often, he chopped down a peanut plant in the action, but he couldn't help that. The kudzu had so entwined itself in places he couldn't separate the enemy from the friend. When Lou called him for lunch, he loaded his weapons in the wheelbarrow and surveyed the battlefield. A good start, he thought with satisfaction.

At that moment he saw someone, or something,

standing in the sea of kudzu leaves, watching him. He stared toward it, toward the point where the leaves had lifted in the breeze just enough to show a figure, watching. His heart lurched. Sweat drops on his forehead turned cold.

Hollis forgot how hot and tired he was. Whirling, he stumbled over the wheelbarrow. For a frantic moment he wanted to lie where he had fallen, concealed by the plants. But he managed to pick himself up and, leaving the load of tools behind, shot up the hill like a rocket propelled by fear. Once inside the gate he locked it and flung himself down in the shade, panting. The dogs surrounded him, looking at him questioningly. When his strength returned and his breathing became normal, he stroked their heads, wishing he could explain to them.

"Come on!" Lou called out the kitchen window. Hollis's bones ached as he hobbled toward the porch.

For the rest of the day he begged off kudzu killing.

Grancy agreed. "That's hard, hot work, but you need to put away the tools in case of rain. Fannie-Dove is very particular that the tools don't rust."

When he asked to take King David with him, Grancy looked surprised. "All right, but put his rope on. He mustn't run loose in the woods."

Holding the rope of a big dog eager to run off while pushing a wheelbarrow loaded with tools uphill and looking over his shoulder to see what might be watching was hard to do. Finally, though, Hollis got the wheelbarrow put away, and he and King David hurried to the house.

Later he wrote several pages in the journal, beginning with the kudzu war. He drew a picture of the vine, three leaves resembling poison ivy. Grancy called it the "foot-a-night vine," he wrote, and he tried to think of a way to test that. He also tried to put into words a description of the green shadowy figure revealed in the kudzu for that one instant. Was it a jealous spirit of the kudzu, a green ghost, or another clue to the secret of the Hollow? He was not sure how he could find out. He was not sure he wanted to find out.

After closing the tablet, he stood at the window, looking down the slope at the peanut patch. The moon shone white-bright, highlighting the log shed, where he had parked the load of tools. But toward Bonepile Hollow, the mass of vines seemed to rustle and hiss as the kudzu snaked its way toward him. Hollis knew he must get out early every day to beat it back into the Hollow where the mysterious watcher hid.

The mouse not coming worried Hollis. The problem, he thought, was popcorn. Preacher Henry, on Saturday shopping trips, had not located any. The grocer said he'd have no more until fall when the new crop was harvested. An idea came to Hollis—somebody along the circle of Dolliver road might have popcorn, either in their kitchen cupboard or in their garden. He determined to find out, not suspecting that his search for mouse popcorn would result in more drastic twists and turns in his already complicated life in the Dolliver woods.

51

8

GRANCY FRETTED over Hollis's request to walk the Dolliver loop in search of popcorn. "You'll get lost," she said.

He reminded her that he couldn't get lost as there was only one road and it made a circle; whichever way he went, he'd always return to her house.

"You can't go to strangers and ask for popcorn," Lou chimed in.

Hollis pointed out that he knew nearly everybody on the loop. Preacher Henry had been coming to Grancy's house every week to bring groceries; the Mayhews were in and out of Grancy's yard nearly every day with berries or fruit from their garden; big Liam had appeared at the door several times to see what they needed done about the house.

"The only stranger is that boy in the sunflower house. And I sure would like to know him. Maybe we could be friends."

Hollis had thought out his arguments well, and he won. He realized that there was a place on the Dolliver loop that no one was mentioning. Only after Grancy yielded did she refer to it. "If you must go, take King David. After you visit that boy, go back the way you went. Don't come past the Bonepile Hollow road."

52

Hollis had planned to look at the gate close up, but he was not too disappointed. If he obeyed Grancy today, maybe she'd let him go again. Then he'd have his chance.

How excited he and King David were to set out on their search. But first he had to get past the spooky cemetery with all the big trees reaching their branches out over the mossy gray stones, almost as if to protect them. Toward the back he could see newer, whiter monuments and the blue-green cedar tree where the Mayhews' son was buried. Feeling uneasy, he and King David crossed to the opposite side of the road.

Now came the covered bridge on his left and Preacher Henry's log house and the church on the right. Hollis already knew Preacher Henry didn't have popcorn, so he stopped at the bridge instead. He could hear the creek rushing past the boulders underneath. He could see the strong thick timbers that had lasted more than a hundred years—since Liam's great-great-grandpa had driven wooden pegs in them. Hollis considered going down under the bridge to look, but he realized that popcorn was his purpose today, and he had to get back by chore time so Grancy would let him come again.

King David led the way to Mayhews'. The prize chickens saw them coming and set up an alarm of cackling and shrieking. Mr. Mayhew popped out of the barn, a pitchfork in his hand.

"I thought some varmit was trying to get in the yard," he shouted above the racket. Hollis felt glad he wasn't a varmit—that pitchfork had sharp shiny tines.

"You got any popcorn?" he yelled.

"Popcorn!" Mr. Mayhew cupped his ear, not believing what he heard.

"I need popcorn," Hollis shouted. "I've GOT to have popcorn."

"Ask my wife." Mr. Mayhew gave a disgusted wave toward the strawberry patch. "Don't let that big dog loose. My chickens won't lay eggs if he chases them."

Hollis held tight to the rope on the way to find Mrs. Mayhew. She was picking berries with both hands and piling them in a basket.

"Have you some," she said without stopping. "Eat all you want."

Hollis bit into a juicy red berry, rolling the rich sweet taste over his tongue. Reaching for more, he said, "Do you have popcorn anywhere?"

"What do you want with popcorn?"

Why was everyone so suspicious about popcorn? "Nothing." He knew that wasn't honest, but how could he blurt out that he needed it for a mouse that sang? It would sound as fantastic to her, standing here in the strawberry patch with the sun shining and the prize chickens cackling, as "immense antediluvian monsters" sounded to him.

When she said, "No, sorry," Hollis and the big dog took to the road again. He saw where Mrs. Mayhew's walking-path to Grancy's entered the woods, on his right. He knew then that next on the right, secluded within a thick wall of green, was Bonepile Hollow. Now to his left stretched Burdock's pasture. That wooly creature stood, head hanging over the fence, staring at Hollis and King David approaching. Hollis felt sorry for the homeless donkey and reached out to pat him. That was a mistake.

Burdock lifted his head and drew back his thick lips in a horrible grin, showing sharp yellow teeth. Fire sparked from his eyes. King David yipped a warning. Hollis jumped away just in time to escape the donkey's snapping jaws. Burdock craned his long neck after them, still clacking his teeth.

Hollis was out of breath when he reached the shade of Liam's yard. Liam, sitting under a big oak, flashed a smile of welcome. "I've been wishing you'd drop by. Did something chase you here?" His black eyes shone like two chunks of coal between bushy black eyebrows and a curly black beard. His polished bald head was ringed with black curls.

"Burdock," Hollis panted. "Why is he so mean?"

"Because somebody's been mean to him." Liam's hands were busy with several hollow sticks of different lengths. Before Hollis could ask another question, Liam added, "I'm making something for you and Rufe."

"Rufe?"

"He lives around the curve where the sunflowers are. About your age. You fellows ought to get to know one another."

"I'd sure like to," Hollis said. "But first I've got to find some popcorn."

Liam cut one of the hollow sticks shorter. "Rufe may have some. He's a great gardener."

Liam's goats stood around in the shade chewing their cuds, big goats, little goats, black, white, and spotted goats. "Pretty goats," Hollis said and, to his surprise, meant it. "Why don't they stink?"

Liam laughed. "I keep them clean. They win ribbons at the fair."

"Neat," Hollis said and started off again.

"Bring Rufe back with you," Liam called after him. "I need to fit you both for what I'm making."

Hollis promised, though he didn't see how anybody could want what Liam was making from odds and ends of hollow sticks.

At the boy's mailbox, Hollis stood a moment, looking ahead to where he knew the Bonepile Hollow gate stood. Grancy's house was not far beyond it. But Grancy had forbidden him to return home that way. He had to circle back the way he'd come. That was all right for today, because Liam wanted to see him and Rufe for some reason. But another day, he hoped to go to that gate and examine those signs and that skull and crossbones.

"What you want?" a voice asked from behind the sunflowers.

"Popcorn," Hollis said. "You got any?"

"Naw, and don't talk so loud. My ma's asleep. And don't let your dog bark." A sandy-haired boy with freckles scattered over his face and a hoe in his hand came across the yard.

"Is she sick?" Hollis asked.

"Naw." Now he was patting King David. "She works the hoot-owl shift. In the coal mine."

Hollis thought that astonishing, but popcorn was more important now. This boy was his last chance. "Don't you have popcorn in your garden, or some you've forgotten in your house?"

"Naw. Want to see my garden?" The boy leaned the hoe against a tree. They went behind the small house. "I'm growing me some watermelons. Look how big!" He separated the leaves to show the long green melons with bright yellow splotches. "They're named Moon and Stars. This big yellow spot is the moon and all these little yellow spots around it are stars."

Hollis admired the melons, then leaned close to Rufe and asked, "What's down in Bonepile Hollow?"

Rufe jumped as if a snake had bitten him. "Shhh! Don't say that!"

"Why not?" Hollis persisted, but talking low. "What's down there?"

Rufe pulled at a blade of grass. "I don't know. Nobody will tell. They just say 'stay away.'"

"Haven't you seen anything? Or heard that awful noise at night? Why is everybody scared?"

Rufe looked all around, the way Mrs. Mayhew had, and whispered, "I've not SEEN anything. But I KNOW something." His voice was like a secret.

Hollis held his breath, hoping Rufe wouldn't suddenly clam up.

"One of Liam's goats got down there. Sharon it was—smartest and purtiest of them all. Liam called her his Rose of Sharon. He'd let me brush her, and we'd polish her horns and shine her little hooves, getting her ready for the fair. She was white and wore a gold chain around her neck, gold like her eyes." Rufe sat still as a stone. Hollis knew he was seeing Sharon in his mind. "She always won the grand prize—the purple ribbon. When she came up missing, we looked and looked. Everywhere. But not in

Bonepile Hollow. Liam didn't want to stir up trouble, he said."

King David sprawled flat in the grass with a sigh. The boys sat down beside him.

"She never came back?" Hollis whispered.

"Never to this day. Nothing that goes down in Bonepile Hollow ever comes out."

Hollis felt a chill hearing these words echoing Mr. Mayhew. "Liam was scared?" He couldn't believe it.

"He wouldn't go. He said worse things would happen to everybody in Dolliver if he did."

They watched a red ant crawling up a weed stem.

"Let's go down in the Hollow and find Sharon," Hollis said.

"You're crazy." Rufe's mouth hung open.

"If anybody catches us, we can say we lost our way."

"Maybe." Rufe sounded doubtful. "But not today."

"No," said Hollis, remembering. "Liam wants us at his house. Now." He nudged King David awake.

At Liam's, the goats still rested in the shade. Their chins moved up and down in regular rhythm. Hollis thought of the white-and-gold Sharon and wished she could be there too.

"I'm making flutes," Liam explained. "I thought you boys needed flutes to play." He showed them how he had cut bamboo fishing poles from the creek bank and measured them into pieces that varied in length. "I let 'em dry," he said, "and now I'm lacing them together in a special arrangement so they'll make music."

"Wow!" Hollis stared in amazement. How could somebody sit in his front yard and make an instrument that produced music?

"Thirteen pipes in each one," Rufe counted. "Every pipe a different length."

"Not only a different length," said Liam, "but, see here, the longer ones are bigger around. As the pipes get shorter they're also smaller in diameter. That changes the sound they make. But the pipes are all even on the topside where you'll blow." Now he finished lacing the bamboo pieces together and handed one to each boy for inspection. "See if your flute fits your hands," he instructed.

"Yeah," said Rufe.

"Just right," said Hollis.

"Your great-granny would call this a panpipe," Liam said. "That's the old-time name for it. I have to tune them and polish them and wax the twine.

Then they'll be ready to play. I'll teach you how."

The boys planned with Liam to come back for the flutes and a music lesson later in the week.

"I've got to fight kudzu tomorrow," Hollis said. "Come and help me, Rufe?"

"Sure. I'll be there soon as Ma gets home from her shift."

With that the boys said good-bye and went their separate ways. Hollis's heart swelled with happiness. He hadn't realized it before, but now he knew it—a flute was what he needed, even more than popcorn. He was remembering that the nature book had said that singing mice were attracted to music. There was that girl who claimed that whenever she began playing the piano, a mouse would come into the light and sing along with the piano. Oh, he would learn to play Liam's flute so he could give a concert for the mouse and bring it back.

This tour of the Dolliver loop had turned out better than he had planned. He was getting a flute that would call back his mouse, he had made a friend who was coming to help fight kudzu, and he had the story of Sharon to add to the Bonepile Hollow clues. He and Rufe would plot an expedition to rescue Sharon, and he would tell Rufe about the watcher in the woods.

As Grancy's house came in sight around the bend of the road, he thought: The only thing that would make me happier would be a letter from Mom and Dad saying they'd made up. Then we'd all be together at home the way we used to be.

The dogs came running to the gate, glad that he and King David had returned. Lou met him at the door with a postcard from Dad—a picture of the Leaning Tower of Pisa—with a scrawled note on the back that said, "I'm thinking of you. Love, Dad."

"Pisa," repeated Hollis. "That's a long way away."

"Yes," agreed Lou. "In Italy."

Grancy said, "Airplanes make short work of long distances."

So Hollis didn't get his perfect morning after all, but near enough for the time being. As Grancy said, "Things can't be mended overnight."

9

NEXT MORNING Hollis awoke to a drumming on the tin roof. Rain! It streaked down so fast and silvery he could barely see the green kudzu beyond the fence. Lightning zigzagged across the sky. Thunder rattled the plunder-room shelves. No kudzu fight today.

He didn't want to go back to bed, and nobody else was up, not even the dogs. Yesterday he had added many pages to his journal, recounting the latest developments. Nothing to do but rummage on the dusty shelves, looking through the old books and cigar boxes of news clippings. One sign, mildewed around the edges, caught his attention because of the big black-printed words followed by eye-popping exclamation marks:

MONSTROUS HYDRARCHOS!

Greatest Sea Serpent Ever Discovered!

WONDER OF THE ANTEDILUVIAN WORLD!!!

☞ *Two Weeks Only* ☜

YOU WILL NOT BELIEVE YOUR EYES!!!!

BASILOSAURUS King of the Lizards!!!!!

!!ZEUGLODON!!

The ad was dated more than a hundred years ago and named a museum in New Orleans as the place where this marvel could be seen for twenty-five cents. Is this Grancy's immense antediluvian monster? Hollis wondered. Is this what's hiding in Bonepile Hollow? He laid the old paper carefully on his bed. Grancy had promised to tell him about the monsters. Maybe if he showed her this, she might tell him today.

About midmorning, to Hollis's surprise, Rufe appeared in the rain. "Ma's sleeping, and I couldn't work in my garden on account of the rain, so I thought I'd come on over here."

Grancy, drinking fruit juice in the big chair, was delighted Hollis had a visitor. "Show Rufe all those old toys in your room," she said. But it was the monster ad that Hollis showed Rufe. "I think it has something to do with Bonepile Hollow."

"Let's ask your great-granny now," Rufe suggested.

Grancy listened intently as they read the notice aloud, taking turns with the lines and sometimes stumbling over the words.

"You're right," she said when they finished. "It is about the bones in the Hollow. But some of it isn't true. The man who wrote that wanted to make money."

"What's true about the bones?" Hollis asked.

"Once the ocean covered all this land. Enormous whales lived here."

"That's hard to believe," Lou said, glancing out the window at the trees and hills.

"What was their name?" Rufe asked, perching on the edge of the bed.

"Zeuglodons they're called today. When they died, their bones settled to the bottom of the ocean and fossilized. Millions of years passed, the water withdrew and left the bones covered with dirt. Soil erosion uncovered some of them, and folks began digging them out."

"They must be whoppers," Hollis said.

"Some zeuglodons were seventy feet long," Grancy said. "That's farther than from here to the mailbox."

"All that was long ago," Lou said. "What does it have to do with Bonepile Hollow now?"

"About a hundred years ago, some of the bones were sold to the man who wrote that ad. He put the bones together the way he thought the whales looked. Then he traveled around the country charging people to see his prehistoric monster."

"A great idea!" said Hollis. "Why can't we see one?"

Grancy hesitated. "Well, the man who owns the Hollow now won't let anyone down there for fear they'll steal the bones. He thinks, too, that the fossils are very valuable and that he can sell them for a fortune when the right buyer comes along."

"I'd buy them," Rufe said. "If I had some money."

"Me too," Hollis agreed, thinking hard to fit what Grancy was saying with the other clues he had collected. "I still don't understand why Mr. Mayhew gets so mad about the Hollow. And nobody will talk about it. Not even you, Grancy."

A shadow crossed Grancy's face. "It's something that isn't easy to talk about—something that's better left unsaid. Help me into my bed, please."

When Grancy was settled among her pillows, she turned her face away from them.

Rufe said, "Look. The rain's stopped. Let's go work on that kudzu."

"How about it, Grancy?" Hollis tugged her little bird-claw hand. He wanted her to come back from wherever her thoughts had taken her. He wanted to see her smile again. "Rufe and I will measure that ole kudzu. We'll see if it really does grow a foot a night."

"Yes," she said with a little smile. "Be sure you let me know if it's true."

The boys took a stake from the plunder room and went to the shed for the wheelbarrow load of tools. They used the heavy froe to pound the stake into the rain-soft ground at the tip of a tendril of kudzu. This time tomorrow they would bring a yardstick, also from the plunder room, and measure how far beyond the stake the vine had grown in twenty-four hours.

While they squatted over the stake, Hollis whispered, "Don't look now," and he told Rufe about the watcher among the kudzu. Rufe kept stealing glances toward the Hollow, as if he couldn't believe what he was hearing.

"I can't figure out if it was real," Hollis continued, "or if it was a shadow. If it was a person or a ghost."

They set to work on the kudzu, staying close together so they could talk and develop their plans. They agreed that they had to go down in the Hollow, not just to rescue Sharon but to see what was down there and to try to fix whatever made Grancy so sad.

It was when they reached the end of the peanut rows nearest the Hollow that they made a stunning discovery—footprints in the muddy ground. Not monster-sized prints, nor even man-sized, but prints slightly smaller than the boys' prints when they compared them. Someone barefoot had been here just minutes ago—since the rain stopped. The boys turned toward the curtain of kudzu draping the trees rising out of Bonepile Hollow. The prints walked into that green curtain.

Hollis and Rufe, without a word, laid down their tools and followed the steps. Once within the forest, the prints disappeared because of fallen leaves and pine needles, but the boys could see a faint path through the shrouded gloom of vines and trees. Silently, they followed it, their noise muffled by the soggy undergrowth. Every so often they paused and listened. At first Hollis could hear nothing because of the hammering of his heart, but the deeper they went, down, down into the Hollow, the quieter he became inside. He concentrated on moving along the path, glancing back occasionally to see that Rufe still followed.

Abruptly, the path ended. At their feet yawned an enormous lake, more like a deep pit, with milky green water reflecting nothing.

"What is it?" Rufe whispered over Hollis's shoulder.

"A lake," Hollis whispered, shifting his position to give Rufe a better look into the depths. A rock dislodged, tumbling down the sheer sides, plunging into the thick liquid with hardly a ripple. If a person fell, or

was pushed, into this pit, there would be no escape, the walls rose so sheer and tall. The water looked as solid and dead as a blank mirror. At the farther end Hollis noticed a gray-white tree branch curving out of the water. It was huge, and near it was an even larger petrified tree stump, barely showing above the opaque surface. The hair on the back of his neck prickled as Hollis realized that these growths had nothing to do with trees. They were bones, ancient bones, rising out of what must have been a pit of bones in times past.

Basilosaurus, King of the Lizards!

Zeuglodons!

The boys gawked, forgetting they were in a forbidden place until a mighty roar, like a bull alligator at mating season, split the still woods. What followed was like listening to an old-time radio program. They heard the sounds, and their minds furnished the actions—a running scream, the thud of a blow being struck, another scream, standing still this time, then a pelting of hard blows, like a fist on a punching bag.

"Don't, don't," pleaded a voice.

"When I tell you to dig, I mean for you to dig," roared the bull alligator voice as Hollis and Rufe threw themselves backward into the sheltering bushes. The noise they made interrupted the beating, and a voice directed toward the pit barked, "Who's there?" In the oppressive silence, the boys heard a sharp, loud click—a rifle being readied for use. Bullets cracked overhead, thudding into the tree trunks around them. They heard angry muttering as something the size of a bulldozer thrashed through the woods toward them.

"Go, go!" Hollis whispered. Crouching low, with flying feet, the boys returned to the peanut patch, trembling from what they'd escaped. What did it mean? They agreed they had found the monster bone pit, monsters dead for millions of years. They had also heard a live monster. Hollis would never forget that voice!

And now they knew there was another person in the Hollow. Hollis feared to meet them, yet he knew that sooner or later, with the plans he and Rufe had made, a meeting was certain. The boys stood whispering among Fannie-Dove's peanut plants till Lou called, "Lunch!"

Rufe couldn't stay. "Ma might be looking for me," he explained.

Hollis walked as far as the mailbox with him. Another card had come from Dad, in Paris this time. "Home soon," he wrote. "Don't forget me." How could they forget him? Every day they talked about Mom and Dad, wondering how things could "work out" with Dad off in Europe. Grancy said going on a trip might be a good thing. "Sometimes it helps folks appreciate what they've got at home," she said.

"I hope so," Hollis said. With all his heart, he wanted their family to be the way it used to be—both his parents, him, and Lou. Sometimes he thought too much about it, and about the mystery in the Hollow that, try hard as he would, he couldn't ferret out, and about the mouse not coming back. He felt like a fired-up cook stove with all the top burners set on high, and the oven on broil. At those times he had to shake himself and remember his new friend Rufe, and the flutes, and measuring the kudzu.

Another thing, Grancy seemed worried about Fannie-Dove. No word had come from her, even though they'd mailed off postcards to her every week. Not the scenic kind like Dad sent from his travels, but plain ones that took a lot of writing to fill the space. Hollis even wrote on one: "I'm taking good care of your pet palm tree." He got the feeling that Fannie-Dove's silence meant something important, else why would Grancy be so concerned?

10

NEXT DAY, at exactly the right hour, Hollis and Rufe measured the kudzu vine. In twenty-four hours it had crawled thirteen inches into Fannie-Dove's peanut patch—thirteen inches closer to Grancy's house. They measured twice to be sure, then moved the stake to the end of the vine again to take another measurement tomorrow.

Grancy clapped her hands when they told her. She suggested they keep a record of each day's growth to see if kudzu grew steadily, or if sometimes it rested. The boys prepared a sheet of paper for their kudzu statistics and kept it on Grancy's bedside table.

Then they were ready to go for their flutes. Grancy and Lou were as excited as the boys, and Lou was doing Hollis's lunchtime chores so he could stay at Liam's for a music lesson.

How fine the flutes looked, Hollis's laced with red twine and Rufe's with blue. They fitted each boy's hands just right. Hollis had thought he would come home a flute-playing expert, but that wasn't the way it happened. They blew and blew and didn't make a note of music. Liam showed them how to pucker their mouths just so, how to blow light and blow heavy, how the tubes of bamboo made different sounds according to how they were blown, and how to use their wind in such a way they never had to gulp for air. Liam showed them all this, but the boys couldn't do it. They kept trying, spit spraying like a mist, till they turned purple and had no more breath. After a couple of hours, Liam said, "Take the flutes home with you and practice. Remember, it's like blowing on a bottle. Pretty soon you'll get the hang of it."

So along the road they went, huffing and puffing and listening to the sounds they blew. Burdock made snuffling noises in his throat when he heard them.

"He's laughing at us," grumped Rufe. Burdock did more than that. Right in front of their eyes he spraddled all four legs, flung up his head, drew back his lips in that terrifying grin, and out of him exploded the ragged, wrenching in-and-out racket that Hollis had heard so many times from the plunder room window. The boys fled, followed by that unearthly cry that canceled one of the most important clues to Bonepile Hollow—the monster scream. Grancy was right! Hollis wouldn't have believed it if he had not seen it happening, and heard it.

At the bridge they decided to lay their flutes in the sun to dry while they climbed down the road embankment to the creek. How good the water felt swirling around their dusty feet and legs. They splashed their hot faces and sank their arms in to the elbows. Soon they were wet all over, so they lay down and rolled.

"Wow!" Hollis said, climbing on a big boulder and jumping in. The boys chased silver minnows, cupping their hands to make a trap, but the tiny fishes escaped with a flick of their tails. Then a water fight developed. Rufe had just splashed a flood of water in Hollis's face when they heard a car roll onto the bridge over their heads. Hollis remembered their flutes. Had they left them too near the road? Would the car smash them? He whirled around and leaped up the embankment.

The car had been coming slowly, but when Hollis appeared out of the bushes, he noticed a change in its sound. The motor revved up, the car's direction shifted. It seemed to take aim, and it came at Hollis full speed. Rufe, climbing the bank behind him, gave a mighty yank on Hollis's wrist and dragged him to safety. The car righted itself, driving on to take the left-hand loop toward Mayhews'.

"He did that a'purpose," Rufe gasped, looking at the trail of dust the car stirred up.

"He sure did," agreed Hollis, relieved to see the flutes safe on a flat rock. He sat down beside them, his knees weak. "Thanks. Whose car was that? Why would anybody want to run over a kid?"

"I don't know whose car it is, but I've seen it pass our house. Have you seen it before?"

"No," said Hollis, thinking hard. "Did you notice the dark windows? Couldn't see who was driving."

"If it goes by my house but not past your house, then it must belong to Bonepile Hollow," Rufe reasoned.

"That means he wasn't trying to run over any kid. He meant to run over me only."

Rufe glanced anxiously toward the road. "Let's go," he said, urging Hollis to his feet. "He might come back."

They trudged past the cemetery, each one thinking about this serious mishap.

"You better tell your great-granny," Rufe said.

"I can't. She's too worried about everything already."

"Tell Liam then. Or Preacher Henry."

Hollis promised, not suspecting that coming events would prevent him from keeping his word.

As Liam predicted, Grancy called the flute a panpipe. She remembered that when she was a child the boys made them. "Sometimes they tied together a double row of cane tubes," she said, feeling the single-rowed flute Liam had made. "The boys I knew made more noise than music."

That was what Hollis did too. Nobody complained about his squeaks and squeals, his heavings and puffings, except the cats always left the room. That worried Hollis. If cats didn't like his music, how could the singing mouse be pleased by it? He struggled to improve. Every spare minute he practiced, between kudzu fighting, household chores, tending Fannie-

Dove's plants, and checking the mailbox for letters from home. He vowed to make his flute produce music.

Rufe stayed busy at his place but dropped over to help Hollis measure the kudzu every day. When they'd kept a record for a week Grancy suggested that they find out the average daily growth. By adding and dividing they found out that their vine on the average grew thirteen-and-a-half inches a day.

After the daily measuring, the boys sat in the porch swing, practicing on the flutes. That's where they were the morning a shiny red sports car whipped around the bend from the bridge and parked outside Grancy's gate. A long-legged girl got out and came in the yard as if she owned it.

"Here's somebody," Hollis called to Lou and Grancy. The boys watched, bug-eyed, from the porch while the dogs raced each other to be first to greet the girl. She stooped to hug them all at the same time. Such barking and whining and jumping for joy Hollis had never seen in his life. The girl—her hair was tan, she was tan, her outfit was white—strode toward them with a wide smile. Hollis knew her instantly—the out-of-focus girl in the picture on the mantel. Josie.

"Where's my great-granny?" She banged through the screen door followed by the dogs and the boys. A great uproar followed—greetings, huggings, barkings. When the hubbub settled, Josie, the five dogs, and two cats were all on the bed with Grancy.

"Why are you in bed? That's what I want to know," Josie demanded.

Grancy was holding Josie's hand. Hollis saw her squeeze it, like a signal, then she said, "It's my summer malady. You know about that. I'll explain my symptoms later." Again that squeezing signal passed between them, then Josie turned to the rest of them.

"I remember you, Hollis," she said, catching his arm and drawing him near. "You were so little, you can't remember me, I know. Look at those eyes. You're an Orr for sure." She put an arm around Lou. "You were always a good helper. I know you're taking proper care of Grancy." Then she gave Rufe a special hug. "You're the image of your pa. How I grieved to hear about his accident."

Hollis saw tears shining in his friend's eyes and for the first time realized Rufe's sorrow.

"Ma's in the mine now," Rufe said. "At night. I worry sometimes, afeard."

"Since the accident, they made the mine safer," comforted Grancy.

Hollis hadn't thought much about Rufe's dad, he'd been so taken up with the thought of losing his own. Rufe didn't talk much about what happened, but he had told Hollis his dad was buried in the cemetery by the church, not far from the Mayhews' son. What would it be like to have your dad dead? Hollis couldn't think about it.

He wished he could remember this strange girl from before. With her tan color, her white teeth, and friendly ways, he liked her right away. He could tell Grancy loved her a lot. Grancy's wrinkled face was beaming. Hollis had never heard her laugh so much. The two of them did most of the talking while those gathered about them listened. The animals seemed to understand everything that was said, looking from Grancy to Josie. Every so often Josie had another round of hugs for everybody, she was so glad to be home.

11

THE FIVE DAYS Josie stayed in Dolliver were the happiest Hollis remembered. All the dark shadows retreated. Even the letter that came from home saying, "No matter how things work out for the two of us, remember we love you both very much," didn't seem too final with Josie there listening. She was fanning Grancy with a pleated fan decorated with peach blossoms, while Grancy lay back on her pillows with closed eyes. Lou refolded the letter and slipped it in the envelope.

"Where are your mom and dad, Josie?" Hollis asked. "Where do you belong?"

"I belong here," Josie said, fanning so fast that fine tendrils of Grancy's hair waved around her face. "Haven't you heard? I was left on Grancy and Grandpa Will's doorstep. I was a throwaway baby."

Grancy's eyes popped open. "Best thing that ever got thrown away in Dolliver," she said, laughing.

Lou looked astonished. "I thought it was a joke about babies being left on doorsteps. Were you really?"

"Just the same as the doorstep," Grancy said. "That day's as real to me now as it was twenty-one years ago, and I could see then as well as you can now. Somebody pulled a new red wagon to the gate and left it, with no note, no nothing except the warm clothes she was wearing. It was a frosty morning, and she gave out a squall to let me know she was there."

"I had fun with that red wagon till it finally wore out," Josie remembered. "It's probably the reason I bought my red car."

"Your coming started a custom," Grancy said. "After that, every unwanted critter turned up in our yard. Dogs, cats, whatever. Remember that skinny mule?"

"And runty little goat," Josie said. "We gave her to Liam. What a beauty she turned out to be."

"The Rose of Sharon," Grancy mused. "With her silky white hair. Her pink hooves. Her polished horns."

In the silence, the clock tick-tocked briskly.

"The critters appeared, and you and Grandpa Will took them in, the same way you did me."

Hollis couldn't get past the news that Josie had been abandoned. "Don't you hate your parents for giving you up?" He looked earnestly into Josie's face.

"I never think of them except to be grateful they left me here." She hugged Grancy. "I miss Grandpa a lot." She went to the fireplace and looked up at the picture. "You painted him just like himself, with that church-deacon face and those jokey eyes."

The clock began its deep bonging of the hour. "I remember helping him build that clock," Josie said. "When I'd hear it striking at night, I thought it had a magic sound. He never let it run down."

"That's my job now," Hollis said. "Every Sunday night I wind the clock—fifteen turns on each side, in the metal holes. Fifteen for the hands to move, fifteen for the strikes, right, Grancy?"

"Right," Grancy echoed. "And you've not forgotten a single Sunday night."

While Josie was there they went fishing in a quiet pool of the creek. They used plump striped worms that Hollis and Rufe picked off the catalpa trees. They caught so many fish they had to throw the smaller ones back. Rufe showed Hollis how to clean the ones they kept. He was a whiz at scaling and gutting fish. "Pa taught me how," he said.

Hollis didn't like that job. The fish were slippery and hard to hold and stuck their fins, sharp as thorns, in his fingers. But how good they smelled in the fry pan, and they tasted even better.

In the afternoons Rufe pushed into the yard a wheelbarrow loaded with Moon and Stars watermelons. Everyone, including Grancy, sat around the picnic table under a shade tree while Josie inserted the wide-bladed knife in the green-and-gold melons. Each one was so sweetly ripe it split open almost by itself.

"You are the best watermelon grower I ever knew, Rufe," said Grancy. Rufe didn't answer, but his grin stretched from ear to ear, and pink juice dripped off his chin.

If rain kept them indoors, Josie brought out Grancy's ragged, stained cookbook, and they browsed through it, searching for a delicious thing to make. Grancy helped them choose because she remembered which recipes had been Grandpa Will's favorites. "Will liked popovers best of all," she said.

"I've not had them in years. Fannie-Dove disapproves of popovers."

Hollis agreed with Grandpa Will—popovers were the best! Josie taught them the secret of making popovers pop so that after she left they could make them for Grancy.

One day, Grancy said, "Have you noticed, Josie, if my Lily-of-the-Palace is in bloom?"

"Let's go see!" said Josie. She and Lou made a packsaddle with their hands, a little seat between them. Grancy sat on the little seat with an arm around each girl's neck, and they walked in every nook-and-cranny of the big yard, telling her about what was growing and letting her smell the flowers in bloom. Hollis followed along, chiming in with his comments, and the dog gang came too, without any rowdiness. They walked with such care it was as if they tiptoed on eggs. They knew that Josie and Lou carried a delicate passenger.

The Lily-of-the-Palace, when they found it, grew out of a green glazed pot in a far fence corner. It had no leaves, but its stout green stalks supported clusters of red blossoms streaked with white; they were big as plates. In the heart of the blossoms, at the base of each petal, lay a smudge of green. They gasped in appreciation, which made Grancy smile. "Is it as beautiful as it used to be, Josie?" Grancy's touch on the flower was light as a butterfly's. "Tomorrow I want you to take it to Grandpa Will's grave. It was his favorite. Every summer he watched for it to bloom."

That's how the flower expedition to the cemetery happened. Rufe came along, bringing marigolds and zinnias for his dad. Lou brought larkspur and petunias for the Mayhews' son, Hollis carried a jug of water, and Josie had the Lily-of-the-Palace carefully in hand. They left the dogs at home to keep Grancy company. Hollis was surprised that Josie and Rufe didn't think of the cemetery as spooky, a place to be afraid. With them, being there was like visiting old friends.

"There's Miss Hattie," said Rufe. "She was my Sunday School teacher."

"Mine too," Josie said with a remembering smile. "She gave us a candy cane for each Bible verse we learned. And here's Mrs. Trotwell. We use to joke about her name."

"She made the best chocolate cakes." Rufe smacked his lips.

"Mr. Verner over there had a pet raccoon that set fire to his house—accidentally, he claimed. Grancy always thought the raccoon knew exactly what it was doing," Josie said.

They came to Grandpa Will's grave. "It's hard to imagine what he was like," Lou said.

"The picture Grancy painted is his mirror image. Those blue eyes were always twinkling." Josie set the Lily-of-the-Palace in place. "He didn't talk much. He carved hickory whistles for me. He liked to sing funny songs." She stepped back to admire the effect of the flower against the gray grave marker. "Ahead of time, he made his own tombstone. See here," Josie pointed. "He wrote this before the cement dried—'Glad you dropped by.' That's what he used to say when people came to visit him."

Now Hollis noticed a place for a grave beside Grandpa Will, and half the stone marked it as belonging to somebody named Emmy Lou Orr. It gave a birth date but no date was beside the word "Died."

"What's this?" Hollis stared at the inscription.

"That's Grancy," Josie said. "Someday she'll be buried here."

"Emmy Lou. That's MY name," Lou exclaimed. "I didn't know it was Grancy's name too."

"You're her namesake. How proud she was when she heard that."

Hollis poked out his lips. "I don't want Grancy to die."

"I don't think she's going to any time soon," said Josie. "But when she does, Preacher Henry will have her funeral in the church, and then she'll be buried here beside Grandpa Will. Folks'll come from miles around."

"I won't!" Red-faced, Hollis stomped his foot.

"She'd want you there," Josie said. "In fact, she'd probably be pleased to have you say something, like a little speech."

"I will," said Lou. "And from this day on, I'm to be called by both my names. I'm Emmy Lou." She announced it to the whole cemetery, Miss Hattie, Mrs. Trotwell, and Mr. Verner included.

Josie adjusted the lily pot a half inch to the right.

"It's beautiful," Lou said, and Rufe agreed. Hollis refused to look, but he did pour water into the pot to keep the lily fresh.

"What did Grandpa Will die of?" Lou asked.

"The doctor said pneumonia," Josie answered.

"But it was grief. Someone he loved broke his heart."

"How? Why?" Lou sounded bewildered.

"Did you ask Grancy about Bonepile Hollow?" Josie asked.

Hollis perked up. "Yes."

"What did she say?"

"She began explaining it," Hollis said, thinking back to that day. "But she hasn't finished yet."

"She will when she's ready. But I will tell you this. There's a monster in Bonepile Hollow, but it's not pre-historic. It poisons dogs, it kills people, it robs graves, but nobody speaks up. They're afraid. So I had to leave. I can't come back till it's not there."

"What you're saying doesn't make sense," Lou said, distressed. "If there's a monster so near, how can Grancy be safe? Who protects her?"

"Grancy's safe, because she's not a blood Orr but an Orr by marriage. The land will never be hers. She just lives on it."

None of this made sense to Hollis either, but be-fore he could form a question they moved on to Rufe's dad. They arranged his flowers with a spray of fern in a jar that was already there. Hollis poured in water.

"That's real purty," Rufe said with satisfaction.

"He's been dead for two years," said Lou, looking at the headstone. "I bet you miss him."

"Yeah," said Rufe. "We used to go fishing a lot in the creek. He showed me how to find Indian stones and signs Indians carved on the rocks."

They stood silent around the grave.

"I may be getting a new dad soon," Rufe said.

"Whatcha mean?" Hollis exploded. "You can't get

a new dad. Nobody can take a dad's place." He felt tears stinging his eyes.

"He won't take my dad's place," Rufe protested. "I won't ever forget Pa. But I'd—I'd like to have some-body—somebody like Liam, to live with my mom and me."

Hollis hurt under his ribs. Yet he knew that Liam would be fun to live with. He didn't know what to say.

Josie touched Rufe's shoulder. "Liam'll be a great dad."

Hollis scuffed up the dirt with his toes and bit his lip. The angry tears that he held back trickled down inside his nose. They moved on to the big cedar where the Mayhews' son was buried. His picture, in Army uniform, laughed up at them from the snow-white marble.

"'World War Two,'" Lou read from under the pic-ture. "'St. Lo, France.' I read about that battle in my history book."

The laughing eyes watched them over the blue larkspur and the pink-and-white petunias.

"I wish I could have known all of them," Lou said.

They made their way out of the cemetery past several chubby angels with their wings unfurled. The church looked quiet and peaceful, waiting for Sunday. Preacher Henry, up on the roof of his house nailing shingles, waved.

At home they reported to Grancy what they had done. Lou announced again that from now on she'd be known as Emmy Lou. Grancy seemed pleased. Josie also had an announcement to make. "I must go back to Memphis tomorrow, early."

Grancy, Lou, Hollis, and Rufe set up such a howl of dismay that King David, asleep on Grancy's bed, awoke. Hollis knew if the big dog could understand what Josie was saying, he'd howl too.

"I'll come back again in the fall, to see Grancy and Rufe," she promised. "Next summer, if Emmy Lou and Hollis are here, I'll see them."

"We'll be here!" they agreed.

Hollis had many things to mull over way into the night. As he listened to the clock striking, he thought about the singing mouse, the flute, and the music lessons. He thought about Josie leaving, and Grandpa Will, Rufe's dad, and the Mayhews' son. He thought about the humongous bones he and Rufe saw in the sinister pit that day they followed the footprints and about the mystery of Bonepile Hollow. A monster alive, Josie had said. "I can't come back till it's not there." How did it all fit together? Grancy was the key. He HAD to persuade her to talk. The more he learned about the Hollow, the less he understood its secret.

He threw off the covers and padded over to the window. Leaning far out, he breathed the damp, earthy midnight air. The low chuckling call of the whippoorwill echoed from the cemetery. There was no moon, only an uncountable number of stars, blue, yellow, white, red. He felt happy and yet sad, a mixture of being here, of having everybody and everything here, yet wishing he were home and everything there the way it had been, the way it once was. How could he know so much but still not understand any of it?

Deep in the woods, toward Mayhews', an owl hooted. Millions of fireflies twinkled in the forest like earthbound stars. He took a last look at the mute shadows of Bonepile Hollow, then hopped into his feather bed. Almost before he pulled up the covers, he fell asleep.

12

A LETTER CAME FROM MOM, making plans for their return in September. Hollis realized summer was flying past. He had to hurry to get done all he wanted to do. He worked overtime on his journal because he hadn't kept it up-to-date while Josie was there. He had to find more clues to Bonepile Hollow so the ones he'd collected would make sense. And the mouse! He must see it once more. He redoubled his efforts on the panpipe. He and Rufe often met at Liam's for a music lesson. Afterwards one day, Hollis didn't go home the long way past Mayhews' and the bridge. Instead he walked with Rufe as far as his house, then continued toward Grancy's by way of the Bonepile Hollow gate. He explained to Rufe that he had to look at those signs up close because of something Josie had said. When Rufe insisted that he explain, he said, "I'll tell you later. I may be wrong."

Off he went, walking briskly but silently along a part of the Dolliver loop he'd never set foot on before. At the point where Rufe's house disappeared behind him and Grancy's house had not yet appeared in front of him, he came to the mysterious gate. At first he stood at the far edge of the road, looking once again at the threatening signs: "KEEP OUT" "NO TRES-PASSING" "GIT BACK!" "THIS MEANS YOU!" Then there was the huge sign that made him catch his breath again, even though he was prepared for it: the white skull and crossbones mounted on a black board. The black was like velvet, and the skull stood out in three dimensions like a human skull, with black eye sockets. Could it be real? That was what he had come to see, because he could not forget that Josie had called the living monster a "grave robber."

He glanced to the left and the right along the road. Nobody. Quickly he crossed to the gate. He stood so close to the skull and stared so hard he could see the grain of the bones. No mistake about it—this was a human skull. The mouth, filled with near perfect teeth, grinned insanely beneath the empty eyes. Hollis peered at the rough road that disappeared downhill into the bushes and woods. The reckless car with the dark windows must have gone down this road. He could see nothing. It was as if a drapery of green closed in the secret. No leaves stirred. He leaned closer against the gate, testing the lock.

In the silence, a sharp loud click sounded, the same noise Hollis and Rufe had heard at the bone pit. Then it had been followed by a spray of bullets raking the woods, with no specific target in sight. Now, the sound was just over the fence in the thick bushes, and Hollis knew the rifle was trained on him.

With a desperate try to save himself, he spun around in the gravel and ran. Any minute he expected to hear the crack of a shot, but he knew that by the time he heard it he would be hit. Frantically he zigzagged, remembering that evasive action made a target harder to hit.

He didn't stop running till he reached Grancy's yard and collapsed in the shade. The dogs crowded around him, wanting to help. When he was able, he sat up, wiped the sweat out of his eyes, and checked the flute to make sure he hadn't damaged it.

Where had that skull come from? He had to find out. Maybe Rufe would have some ideas. Tomorrow! With the summer almost over, he and Rufe had to make their scouting trip down the Hollow road. There had to be a house down there, a place for the monster to live and to keep his car.

For the first time, Hollis felt undecided. Whoever cocked that rifle—at the pit and at the skull gate—meant business. He didn't want Hollis to know about the skull, didn't want him to know what was in the Hollow. Hollis's mind formed the words Mr. Mayhew had spoken the first day in Dolliver and Rufe had echoed later: "What goes down into the Hollow never comes out again." From what he had learned, he was finally convinced that was true. And now he felt afraid.

That fear caused the boys later to postpone their sneak trip into the Hollow and instead search for the source of the skull and bones posted at the gate.

"Grave robber!" Rufe gasped. "I remember Josie said that but I didn't notice it at the time."

Now the boys took extra care when they were out and about. The instant they heard a car along the road, they dived off into the bushes. They stayed away from the skull gate. Their new plan was to leave Liam's as soon as their lesson ended and head for the cemetery. They wandered through every inch of it looking for a disturbed grave. They stayed together but went over the cemetery in an orderly way, taking a fourth of it each time they went. Everything was as it should be. Some of the graves were covered with little houses, some were boxed up with crumbling bricks, some were like Grandpa Will's and Rufe's dad and the Mayhews' son. All of them were intact.

The last day of their search, they stood at the back edge, where there were no more graves because of the woods.

"What's next?" asked Rufe. "Where else would he find a skeleton?"

"Dunno," Hollis said, turning to look into the woods while his mind worked over the problem. As they puzzled what to do, the sun shone through the trees at just the right angle to reveal a strange thing—a fancy iron fence, so rusted it at first appeared like more shadows. The boys moved into the woods as if at a signal. They tore aside bushes that blocked the way to what turned out to be an old fence enclosing several graves. A gate with iron leaves decorating it hung on one hinge. The tombstones were tilted and broken. The graves were overgrown with briars. But the boys saw immediately a pile of earth with a long, narrow hole beside it. Silently, they made their way into the enclosure, and squatted beside the hole, pushing apart the vines to see better. Water stood in the bottom, down about twice the length of the yardstick Rufe and Hollis had used to measure kudzu.

"About six feet deep," Hollis whispered.

"Just right for a grave," Rufe whispered back.

"Been a while since it was done, according to how these vines have grown."

They pieced together the shattered grave marker.

"What's J-n-o-? John?" Hollis said.

"Yeah. Mims. John Mims. Looks like he died in 1830."

"At age thirty-six," Hollis deciphered. "You ever hear of any Mimses?"

Rufe shook his head. "But folks must have forgotten these graves are here."

The sun went behind a cloud, casting a deep shadow over them. All at once they realized where they were and what a horrendous thing they had discovered.

"Let's get out of here," Hollis whispered. Rapidly they left the old graves behind as they headed through the cemetery for the open space of the road. There they slowed down.

"We've got to tell somebody," Rufe said. "Did you ever tell about that wild car? Or about the rifle?"

"I've not had time. Josie came, and we had so much else to do—" He explained he was writing down the evidence so he wouldn't forget anything.

"This is getting too scary," Rufe said.

"I know," Hollis agreed. "But I don't want to worry Grancy or make her feel bad." He hesitated. "The main thing is, she'd keep me home so we could never find out what's back of all this."

"We could tell Liam and ask him not to tell your great-granny."

"But once we tell anybody, Grancy's going to hear about it, no matter what."

They came into Grancy's yard, where the joyful dogs welcomed them. Under cover of the noise, they decided that Hollis should make a listing of all the clues that he had collected, and the two of them would take the list to Liam tomorrow.

The boys practiced on their flutes till chore time. Hollis made the list for Liam after supper by the light of the big flashlight.

Early the next day Rufe came to Grancy's with a troubled face. "Liam's not home today. He won't be back till tomorrow. I'm looking after his goats."

That meant Rufe had to take care of his place and Liam's. Hollis was way behind with his share of taking care of Grancy. This unexpected change of plans gave him time to help Lou, who doubled up for him when he and Rufe went on their jaunts.

"Are you watching the peanut patch?" Grancy asked while Hollis was braiding her hair that mid-morning. "That sneaky kudzu will take over if you're not careful."

Hollis promised he'd see about it first thing to-morrow. He and Lou had a big wash to do besides the routine chores and letters to write for themselves and Grancy. And always there was flute practice. His hope of calling back the musical mouse one more time before he had to leave Dolliver kept him trying. He blew, and he blew, sitting in the porch swing outside Grancy's window. He forced some of the air down in the tubes and sent some of the air skimming across the tops. He discovered he could lengthen the notes and swerve them and make them tremble or dance and skip. He could make them sound like a trolley tootling down the line or like a nightbird calling from deep in the woods.

This day Grancy called through her window, "I could dance a jig to that tune, Hollis. You're sounding real musical."

It was all he needed to know he was ready to present the mouse concert.

13

THAT NIGHT the moon was full. It shone in at the plunder-room window like a beacon, highlighting Fannie-Dove's palm. Hollis had spread a feast for the mouse tonight—peanuts, bacon, cheese, and biscuits. Then he seated himself cross-legged on the floor like a snake charmer and began to play. At first he thought only of getting the panpipe to make the notes, but as he sat there in the shadow, watching the moonlit tree and feeling the warm woodsy breezes that blew in the window, he began thinking of this summer in Dolliver. Without understanding how it happened, he heard his thoughts becoming the music—Grancy and her old house and Grandpa Will; King David and the other dogs, and Thompkins and Samantha; his friend Rufe, and Josie and Lou and Preacher Henry and Liam and the Mayhews, Bonepile Hollow and the covered bridge and the cemetery.

On and on he played, forgetting why he was playing till a small shadow flicked under the palm, and he knew the mouse had come back. He stopped playing to watch the little creature eat in the beam of the flashlight. After it washed, Hollis picked up the panpipe again, hoping the mouse would make a duet with him. And so it did, standing on its hind legs, chest thrust out, head back. It warbled and trilled, and so did Hollis, thinking his heart would burst.

At last his lungs could pump no more air and he had to lay down the flute. But the mouse sang on and on. When its song was finished, it nibbled another snack, then disappeared in a wink. Hollis sensed a finality about tonight. The mouse would not be back. He extinguished the light and rose stiffly from the floor. Without a sound he crept to the feather bed and rolled in.

Moonlight suffused the room, softly enfolding all the plunder stacked there from Hollis's ancestors. Outside the window he could hear the woods rustling and murmuring and the kudzu creeping. The clock Grandpa Will had built of cherry wood began striking, mellow and deep, sounding to his ears just the way it had sounded to Josie when she was growing up in this house. He never heard the clock finish. For some reason he did not know, Hollis turned his face into the bolster and cried in a way that he had never cried in his life. "Oh, Mom! Oh, Dad!" he sobbed. "Grancy! Grancy!" When his crying storm passed, he fell into an exhausted sleep, hugging the bolster.

14

GRANCY ASSIGNED HIM to the peanut patch the next day. Hollis could see that since he was there last, the kudzu had silently moved toward the house, recovering much of the ground that he had cleared. Could he ever win over it? He had to! If the peanut patch disappeared under the kudzu, next would be Grancy's house. He set to work. While he whacked vines he kept an alert eye toward Bonepile Hollow. He had developed a new plan. If he saw something spying on him, he would confront that something to find out who or what it was. What bothered him most about that plan was the possibility that the being watching him might be a ghost of some kind, or the guardian of the kudzu. How would he handle that?

Hollis kept glancing toward the mass of leaves shrouding the trees in Bonepile Hollow while he slashed, chopped, pulled, and cut. Today there was something different about the green wall of kudzu. What puzzled him he couldn't tell, because he didn't dare look directly that way. But the vines were disturbed—they didn't hang in their usual way. His heart gave a peculiar lurch when he realized the watcher was there. He remembered his careful plan as he clipped and chopped his way closer to it. He forced himself to move unhurriedly.

Clip, chop, pull, cut. The watcher appeared to be wearing a sun hat, but it stood in the shadows. Clip, chop, pull, cut. He must pretend not to see it for his plan's success depended on surprise.

When he reached the edge of the peanut patch nearest the apparition—clip, chop, pull, cut—he suddenly threw down his mattock with a ghastly shriek and sped toward it. Just as he had hoped, the watcher was stunned by his bloodcurdling scream and sudden action, and couldn't move. That allowed Hollis to cover half the space separating them despite the kudzu writhing and coiling about his legs to hinder him.

Hollis imagined himself a slippery eel slithering through an ocean of green seaweed. That way he almost reached the watcher before it whirled and fled. It was no ghost—Hollis heard flying feet thudding the ground, and branches and vines crashing and ripping. He sped into the green-draped forest after it. Racing along between high banks of kudzu was like going through a long tunnel because the trees, hanging with vines, closed in overhead. He could no longer hear those rapid, running steps above the sound of his own panting, but he passed a ragged straw hat beside the trail. The speedster ahead of him had lost its hat but was too afraid to stop and pick it up. That gave Hollis courage. Knowing that the watcher was more afraid than he was put wings to his heels.

That's when Hollis let his guard down. That's when the huge leg and foot thrust out from the vines and tripped him. He was going forward at such a speed that the sudden obstacle sent him somersaulting through the air to crash against the kudzu. He fell so hard his neck would surely have broken if the vines hadn't cushioned him. Hollis blanked out.

15

ROUGH HANDS jerking him to his feet brought back Hollis's senses. He tried to twist around to see his captor while he fought to get loose. "Let me go!" He kicked and tried to bite, but powerful arms and huge hairy hands locked him in place, his back against an enormous body that stank of old sweat and tobacco juice. Was this the live monster Josie spoke of with such loathing? The one he and Rufe heard that day at the bone pit? It wasn't the watcher he had chased, he was sure. It was too big, too strong.

His captor spoke no word, only carted Hollis, locked securely in its embrace, toward a clearing where he could see great piles of bones every-where—jaw bones with huge teeth in place; rib bones curving like barrel staves, except bigger; backbones the size of tree trunks; huge skulls with long alligator-like jaws studded with teeth. A bone yard for real.

At last he was in the heart of Bonepile Hollow, but this wasn't the way he had meant it to be. He strained his eyes to take in everything he could without letting the monster know he was looking. Bones, bones, bones. Ahead lay an orchard of bedraggled fruit trees with the huge bones piled along the back edge like a high fence. Near it sat a house on what looked like a foundation of backbone joints.

His captor headed for an outbuilding near the house. It too sat on chunks of bone. Hollis thought how grim it would be living among these mountains of bones in this valley smothered with kudzu. He could smell the bones, calcified powder mixed in hot dust that rose from the huge boots of his captor as it strode toward the shed. Not once did the monster loosen its tight clasp. Hollis could barely breathe.

He caught sight of a boy then, the size and shape of the watcher, peering round the corner of the house. Hollis forgot and turned his head sharply to take a closer look. His captor, with a muttered curse, shifted Hollis into the grasp of one powerful arm and covered his face with its other hand. Before blackness blotted out the scene, Hollis clearly saw a boy about his size, unhappy eyes bulging in his pinched face, wearing a faded shirt and tattered shorts. His skinny body hunched over as if he hurt, and his knobby feet were bare.

Then the monster hurled Hollis into the shed with such force the wind was knocked out of him in a loud whoosh! He lay on the dirt floor looking up, up, at a towering man in overalls. The man laughed down at Hollis, a laugh that was not funny or happy, but threatening. It made Hollis's hair rise like a dog's hackles.

"I warned you to keep away," the man gloated. "That day at the gate. You thought I didn't mean it!" He nudged Hollis hard with his heavy boot. Hollis's leg jerked in terror. The man laughed again, showing his yellow teeth that reminded Hollis of Burdock's snapping jaws.

But what scared Hollis worst of all was the sight of the face bent over him—the same face that looked down from Grancy's mantelpiece, with the straight mouth enclosed on each end with parentheses wrinkles, the arched nose with intense blue eyes set on each side—the face of Grandpa Will! Grandpa Will who was dead and buried in the Dolliver Church cemetery with Grancy's Lily-of-the-Palace decorating his grave. Grandpa Will who was loved by Grancy and Josie.

The man seemed to read Hollis's struggling thoughts, because he laughed again, a laugh that said as plain as words, "I'll tend to you later." He gave Hollis another painful kick before turning away. The last things Hollis heard as he faded into darkness were the rattle of the door latch being locked in place and the man's heavy footsteps receding.

21ST CENTURY ACADEMY SCHOOL

16

WHEN HOLLIS became conscious again, he lay still for a long time, listening. He heard doors slamming and a hoarse voice bawling some name like "Roy." It sounded as if the monster-man was searching for somebody in the house. Slowly—because his body ached—Hollis got up from the hard floor. He tried to find a peek hole in the wall so he could spy on the house, but the wood was solid. He pushed on the locked door, trying to open a crack wide enough to see outside. The door wouldn't budge.

Suddenly, he heard the man, with a ferocious roar, find what he was looking for. Then he heard the sharp smack of a cane on bare skin and the wordless cries of the someone being whipped. It was like standing on the brink of the bone pit that day, except now Hollis knew who was getting beaten—the thin, ragged boy. The beating seemed to go on forever as Hollis cringed against the door, feeling the pain of each blow.

Finally, the man growled, "That'll teach you to meddle with those folks! I told you to let them alone!" The rough voice was hateful to Hollis's ears. He held his breath, listening for those heavy steps. But then the cane clattered to the floor and silence took over Bonepile Hollow.

Hollis tried to sort out his thoughts, to get them in order. His mind hadn't caught up with what had happened. One minute he was fighting kudzu to save the peanut patch and Grancy's house, and the next minute he was locked in a shed in this forbidden place by a madman. What would Grancy and Lou think when he didn't come home? How would they know what had happened to him? Mr. Mayhew had said that things that went down into the Hollow never came out. Rufe had said it too. Now he was down in the Hollow. What chance did he have of coming out of it alive?

Nausea made his stomach heave. Why hadn't Grancy told him that Grandpa Will was the monster of the Hollow? Josie — he felt sick to think Josie had fooled him too. But maybe she didn't know. But she must. Who was buried in Grandpa Will's grave? Was it empty? The argument raged in his head like a fever, with Hollis struggling to keep his trust in two people he had come to love. He could not believe that either Grancy or Josie had lied to him. There had to be some other explanation, and he would never know what it was if he didn't escape.

As Grancy would say, he'd better stir his stump and find a way out of this prison. The walls, built of strong boards, were unyielding, at least along the part that he could reach. Junk filled the back half of the room, but there was nothing he could use to chop through a board or to dig in the hard-packed dirt floor under the wall.

But he knew he had to get out. He couldn't imagine what the monster planned to do with him, but it was dangerous to hang around and find out. He prowled the windowless enclosure, examining everything he came across, desperately thinking of plans and discarding them.

He found a musky-smelling pile of white fur with a jumble of bones and a skull topped with an elegant set of polished horns. Liam's prize goat—all that was left of the Rose of Sharon. Near the base of her skull a dull gleam caught Hollis's attention—the gold chain that matched Sharon's eyes. He took it from the rancid heap and put it in his pocket. If he ever could get free, he would at least have the chain for Liam.

Sharon had starved or died of thirst in this hut. Knowing that the same fate awaited him, Hollis seized Sharon's biggest bone, shuddering at the ragged bits of dehydrated meat clinging to it and the putrid odor, and searched for a likely place to tunnel under the wall with it. But the bone could not dent the stone-hard dirt.

It didn't matter anyway. Tossing the bone aside, Hollis sank to the floor. No way out. He had to stay in this hot, dim building. And wait. Strange that he could be so wet with sweat and yet so thirsty. His fingers, rough and bleeding from slivers, and black with dirt, shook as if he had a chill. Yet the sun's heat radiated from the tin roof, pressing him flat like a blanket of iron. He could not tell how long he lay there almost in a trance when he heard a slight noise, more than a mouse would make, toward the back of the shed and up high. Without moving his body, he turned his head in that direction and watched, fascinated, as a corner of the tin roof trembled, then lifted, and an eye looked in at him.

17

HOLLIS BLINKED. What was it? The eye vanished and a hand appeared, beckoning him to come. He could hardly move, but he forced himself to sit up. He realized that no way could he climb that junk pile and reach the roof corner, even if he wanted to. And he wasn't sure he wanted to. A rescue? Or a trap? He didn't know. But wouldn't anything be better than lying helpless in the shed waiting for the monster to return? Arguing with himself was no help.

He pushed his board-stiff body upright, every bone protesting with pain. He forced himself to walk, then to lift his leg and start climbing over old washing machines, automobile motors, truck tires, bags full of jars and trash. Cans clanked. Guiltily he glanced up at the roof corner. He could see pale lips forming "Shhhh!" with a thin finger against them for quiet. Hollis knew he must not make a sound to call attention to the shed and what was going on here.

Panting with strain, he reached the top of the junk pile and squinted his eyes to look outside. Green leaves. A swatch of blue sky. Then the boy's bony face with the big eyes moved back into view, not a foot away.

"You got to get yourself up in this corner and squeeze through," the face whispered. "Suck in your breath. Make yourself as teensy as you can. I'll hold up the tin and help you out on this limb."

Hollis lost hope. The space from the top of the junk heap to the hole in the roof measured as high as his head. How could he climb straight up a sheer wall?

"Catch hold of here," the voice whispered. "Then come right on up like a monkey."

Hollis stretched up on tiptoe, straining to clutch the thick board the tin roof rested on. Heaving and pushing, trying to tear loose from gravity, he finally raised one leg high enough to get his foot stuck through the hole. He could no longer see the boy, but he heard his whisper: "While I raise the tin now you come on out, like a snake going tail first into a hole. But HOLD ON tight." The boy must have known how Hollis was trembling. The sky seemed to open up directly above Hollis as he hauled himself over the ledge, slithering through the opening exactly like a snake. He turned his body over so that he was holding on by his arms and chest with his legs dangling on the outside.

"Now ease on down till you find the limb. I'm holding onto you." The tin roof lowered without a sound. Hollis felt a hand grasp his jeans, steadying him. He reached all around with his feet searching for secure footing. At last he found the limb. He leaned his head against his arms, too tired to move. His hands still held onto the board at the top of the wall, with the warm tin of the roof lying on them.

"Leggo now and hold onto me," the boy said from behind Hollis.

One of the hardest things he ever had to do was turning loose that board and trusting the strange boy to keep him from falling.

"Get astride of the limb now, and lay down and follow me like an inchworm."

Slowly, like caterpillars, they crept along toward the stout trunk of the tree. Then they descended limb by limb toward the ground, which Hollis couldn't see yet because of the thick leaves tossing in the wind. How glad he was that the leaves hid them from any spying eyes.

The boy below him stretched his skinny body from limb to limb easily, but Hollis sometimes needed help. They came down to earth behind the shed, where they couldn't see the house. The most enormous bonepile of all—Mt. Everest, it seemed to Hollis—cast its shadow across them. All sizes of bones were thrown carelessly together in a mountain that reached an unsteady height, disappearing among the leaves above them. It looked as if it might topple any second. Hollis shivered. His legs gave way, and he sank to the ground.

For the first time, he looked squarely at the boy. Hollis knew that he was the same one who had watched the monster throw him in the shed, but how different he appeared since his beating—now his swollen bloodshot eyes, the angry welts criss-crossing his arms and legs encrusted with blood shocked Hollis.

"How did you know about the roof?" he whispered, wishing he could let the boy know how sorry he was about the beating.

"I made the hole. He's locked me in there lots of times and forgot about me. But quick—you got to go." He pulled Hollis to his feet.

He tried to stand straight but had to cling to the other boy. "You'll get in trouble again, won't you?" Hollis shuddered to think of another beating.

The boy shrugged. "Maybe not. Won't be nothing new if I do. He might forget though."

"Did he forget Liam's goat?"

"Naw. He did it on purpose."

"He's crazy," Hollis whispered fiercely.

"Shhhh! You don't know what crazy is till he hears you say that! Just go! Go!"

108

Hollis caught his arm. "Come with me!"

A door slammed. The wind or the monster?

"He'll kill me!" The boy gave Hollis a shove. "Run!"

Hollis heard the panic in his voice and saw his eyes bulging with terror. "Keep low behind the bonepiles. Hurry!" The boy disappeared in the opposite direction.

Hollis dropped to all fours and headed toward the tunnel of kudzu that led to the peanut patch.

18

BUSHES SHIELDED HIM from the house till he reached the bone fence that ran the length of the orchard. Now he could stand up and cover ground faster because he was well hidden. He still kept his head low and made as little noise as possible. The distance between the shed and the woods seemed endless, and the pieces of bone underfoot rattled loudly no matter how carefully he placed his feet. Any moment he expected huge hairy hands to clamp hold of him and enormous hard boots to trip him. And that ugly, grating voice! Hollis hoped he would never hear it again.

He redoubled his efforts to climb the hill to safety. How great it felt to finally emerge from the kudzu near Fannie-Dove's peanut patch. The wilted vines he'd cut, the tools scattered around the wheelbarrow—he had thought he'd never see them again. He could hardly lift his feet, but the sight of the yard gate with all the dogs anxiously looking through at him gave him a surge of power that carried him into the yard. King David ran toward the house with an alarm bark that seemed to command: "Help Hollis! Hurry!"

"Lou!" Hollis croaked. "Grancy!" He brushed past the other dogs and headed for the porch. He knew he was torn and bleeding and dirty, but he didn't know

110

how awful he looked until his sister, hurrying down the steps to meet him, turned pale and cried out, "Hollis! What happened? Where have you been?" She helped him into Grancy's room.

"Water!" he gasped, collapsing in Grancy's big chair.

"What's the matter?" Grancy's face went white as her hair, and she lay still as one of the jaw bones in Bonepile Hollow.

He gulped down the water Lou brought. "More," he begged.

"No, no!" Grancy forbade. "Later. You mustn't drink too fast. Tell us!"

"We thought you slipped off with Rufe," Lou said, bathing his hot face with a wet towel. "Where were you?"

Stumbling over the words, he told them what had happened. He couldn't tell things in order, and he couldn't think of everything, but he could see the effect of his story on Grancy. She shrank smaller and smaller in the big bed, and her face looked as if every word he spoke hit her like a fist.

Suddenly he ran out of words except for the most important ones that had been beating in his brain ever since he'd looked up from that dirt floor into the face of the monster. "That man—that monster—" He leaned toward Grancy and almost shouted, "He is the man in the picture—the one you painted—Grandpa Will!"

19

─ ◂

"THAT DEVIL is not your Great-grandpa Will." Grancy's jaws clipped her words like a machete. "He's Will's brother, Wibb. Born in this house. Grew up here. Orphans they were, so Will always looked out for his baby brother. They went everywhere together, did everything together, planned everything together." Her thin hands held to each other so hard the knuckles stood up white and lumpy.

"What happened?" Lou asked, daubing Hollis's cuts and scratches with something that stung. "Why did Wibb turn bad?"

"The bones," Grancy said. Hollis could tell how hard it was for her to say the words. "And me."

He wanted to shout, "Go on! Tell!" but he forced himself to hold still.

After a while she said, "The bones were part of their farm. The brothers plotted how they'd make a fortune selling them. Then Will happened on something that made him forget the bones and the money—me. We married, and Will brought me here to live." Her voice sank so low Hollis had to lean forward to hear.

"Wibb went wild. He tore the place apart, saying he and Will didn't need anybody else in their lives, that Will was a traitor to the Orr blood. When Wibb saw he couldn't make Will send me away, he moved out of this house. Built that bone house in the Hollow. Claimed all the bones for himself."

Lou moved to Grancy's bed and took her hand. "How awful for you."

"But Will never blamed me. He said there was no reason he couldn't have his wife and his brother. He always tried to make peace with Wibb. But Wibb grew meaner and meaner. From that bone house he slipped around Dolliver stealing things—animals, tools, boats—whatever was unguarded. And slashing tires. He stole Burdock and mistreated him so bad even Wibb's scared of him." Grancy picked at a thread in the white counterpane. "He played cruel tricks on Will. He wanted Will to die so he could be sure the bones were his alone. Anyone who might inherit Will's right to Bonepile Hollow, he wanted them dead too."

Now Hollis knew why Grancy was so concerned for his safety, why she would never let him wander around Dolliver alone. Someday the bone pit would be his!

"Why didn't Wibb sell the bones?" Hollis asked.

"He couldn't find a buyer, so he never made the fortune he'd dreamed of. Bitter he was, and full of hate toward Will." Grancy lay silent, gathering strength to say, "Will finally broke under the constant hatred from the brother he loved, the one who was like his other self." She swallowed hard. "Will determined to make peace with Wibb. He went down in the Hollow. . . . I begged him not to go. I suspected—" She seemed unable to find the words she needed. She swallowed and started over again. "But I didn't know how deep Wibb's hatred went, deep enough to beat Will unconscious and push him into the bone pit. When Liam found Will, he was all but dead.

"We laid him in this bed. He called his brother's name with every breath he took. To give him peace, Josie vowed to fetch Wibb. By herself she went through the night woods to roust Wibb out of bed. He refused to come. He laughed and told Josie to get off his property or he'd use her for target practice." The cherry-wood clock ticked loud in the stillness. "So Will died, his heart unmended. Pneumonia, the doctor said, but we knew different. At the last, Will made me promise that no harm would come to his brother."

"Wibb must be crazy," Lou whispered in the heavy silence.

"He's sick in his mind. All of Dolliver knew it, but we were too afraid of him to take action. More than that was my promise to Will." Grancy seemed to gather her thoughts and make up her mind. "But a promise can't stand in the way of saving that boy. Emmy Lou, run to Preacher Henry's. Tell him to bring Mr. Mayhew and Liam. Right away! Hollis will tell them what happened. Then we'll decide what's to be done. That boy—I can't rest till he's safe."

As Lou hurried out the door, Grancy called, "Take the dogs with you. Keep alert." Hollis knew this last order was a measure of Grancy's fear—to send all the dogs to protect Lou, and none of them leashed.

Soon the three solemn-faced men gathered round Grancy's bed, listening to Hollis repeat his story.

114

Then Hollis took Sharon's gold chain from his pocket and handed it to Liam.

"Yes, it's hers," he said after one grim look.

"Where would Wibb Orr get a boy?" Grancy asked.

"Stole him, I'd guess," Liam said. "The way he did everything else."

"Talking to Wibb won't change him—we've tried that," Preacher Henry said.

"Time for talking is past." Mr. Mayhew's words came in jerks, like hiccups. "We have to DO something once and for all." His face puffed red the way Hollis remembered it the first day in Dolliver.

"Call the sheriff!" Liam said in his deep voice. "Whatever we do must be done according to the law so it can't be undone. Mrs. Orr, you are the only one who can sign papers committing Wibb Orr to the mental hospital."

Grancy ran her tongue over her dry lips, and a helpless look came over her face. Lou took her hand.

"It's hard to put my husband's brother under lock and key. Will loved him. Will died trying to help him. And I promised—"

They waited while Grancy lay in the sightless dark, thinking. When she spoke again, her voice rang out, startling them. "Yes. I must."

"He'll get treatment," Preacher Henry assured her.

Grancy lifted her chin. "I'll sign the papers."

"That'll be required later," Liam said. "Right now we've got Hollis's complaint and this Roy in danger, so there's reason enough for Wibb to be locked up."

Preacher Henry stood. "I'll call the sheriff from

my house. We'll go with him—Hollis too—and confront Wibb."

After that, events moved fast. The sheriff thought action against the Bonepile Hollow monster long overdue. "I wondered how far you Dolliver folks were going to let Wibb push you with his deviltry. As long as everybody pretended nothing was wrong, my hands were tied."

"It was Hollis," Grancy said, "who made us face up to the truth. We can no longer ignore what's happening even if it is one of our own who's doing it."

20

WHEN THE TWO CARS—Preacher Henry's and the sheriff's—drew up to the skull gate, Hollis felt unreal. Here he was going through that dread barrier that had challenged him for so long. Liam cut the locked chain with nippers, and the gate creaked open.

"Prop it back," the sheriff said quietly. "Just in case we have to leave fast."

"If things go wrong and we can't get Wibb, at least snatch the boy," said Liam.

In the silence before they got back in the cars, a slow, rumbling crash reverberated from the Hollow. Muffled echos wavered through the forest. They looked at each other.

"Hurry!" urged Hollis.

As the cars bumped down the overgrown road, he trembled inside. What was that ominous, rumbling roar? Would Roy be safe? Hollis was not afraid for himself. He knew he would be all right here in the car with Preacher Henry and Liam. He watched the car ahead with the silhouette of Mr. Mayhew sitting beside the sheriff. What would they find at the end of the road?

They drove out into the clearing. There was the high bone wall by the orchard that had hidden him when he escaped. There was the shed with its locked door and the big tree towering behind it. There was the house with closed shutters squatting on its bone foundations. Everything seemed the same except for the milky white air that was gritty with dust.

Nothing living was in sight.

The sheriff parked at the bone steps of the house. He got out, leaving the car door open, and came back to them. "I'll try to raise somebody. Meantime you all stay put so he won't panic at such a crowd."

Nobody answered his pounding. Then he called out, "Wibb Orr? Halloooo, Mr. Wibb!" He tried the door. It swung open. The others waited in tense silence while the sheriff went through the house calling. Nobody. No response.

"The shed," Hollis said. "Roy may be locked in the shed."

The men smashed the lock and jerked the door open. The fetid odors, the dank moldy junk, sickened Hollis. It was just as he had last seen it, and Roy was not there. They walked around the outside of the shed to the escape tree. Nothing had changed there either, except the mountain of bones had toppled and spread out.

"Look at that!" the sheriff exclaimed. "Acres of bones! Did you ever see so many in your life?"

"It was a lot taller when Roy helped me down the tree," Hollis said.

They stared, awestruck. Here was Wibb's fortune, unclaimed by any buyer. Silence closed in on them, a dead silence.

"Where is Roy?" Hollis felt anxious for his friend.

118

"Think hard," Liam urged. "If he's scared and hiding, where could he be?"

Hollis's eyes rested on the rescue tree, its huge trunk so solid, its thick leaves so concealing. Quickly he moved to it, looking at the dense foliage overhead.

"Give me a boost," he said, and up the tree he went to the first big limb. As he climbed higher, he paused to listen. At last he heard something—frightened breathing in the mass of leaves above him. Hollis continued to struggle upward. At the bough that reached the escape hole in the shed roof, Hollis saw clinging close as a shadow against the tree trunk a ragged scrap of faded shorts and a fast-holding bony hand.

"Roy," he called softly. "It's me, Hollis. Are you all right?"

Silence. Nothing moved.

"Roy, my friends are here. We've come for you."

Hollis heard a long tremulous sigh. "No use o'you coming now. It's too late."

Hollis faltered, "What do you mean? Where's the monster?"

"That's what I mean." Roy slowly came out of hiding and looked down at Hollis with swollen eyes. Angry red wounds streaked his cheeks and arms. "I done killed Mr. Wibb."

Hollis felt relief. "Then we're safe. Come on down." He backed down the tree, Roy hesitantly following.

On the ground Roy looked with big eyes at the sheriff. "You come to jail me?"

"No, no," said the sheriff. "Where's Mr. Wibb?"

"There." Roy pointed a trembling finger at the collapsed mountain of bones.

The sheriff looked puzzled. "Just take your time and explain. Tell us what you mean."

Hanging his head, Roy said so low that Hollis could hardly hear him, "Mr. Wibb's dead—I killed him."

21

"I KILLED HIM," Roy repeated, thick-tongued. "I didn't mean to. He—wh-whipped me. Locked me in the shed." He paused. They waited without moving. "I thought he'd gone. So I climbed out the way I showed him." He gestured toward Hollis. "But Mr. Wibb caught me. He said—said—" Roy swallowed hard like a great lump obstructed his throat. "To come down outta the tree, that he was gonna teach me a lesson I'd never forget." Roy stood first on one bare foot, then the other.

Liam clasped him round the shoulders. "Go on," he said gently.

"I was scared to death. I wouldn't come down. He came up after me and was dragging me down. I hung onto a limb and kicked him hard as I could. He musta been dizzy or something 'cause he just pitched out of the tree backwards into the bonepile."

"The bones covered him over," the sheriff said.

Roy nodded.

"Did it happen just now?" Preacher Henry asked.

Roy nodded again, looking at the ground.

"That roar we heard when we stopped at the gate," Liam said.

"Let's get to work," said the sheriff, shucking his uniform jacket and tossing his hat onto a standing bone like a hat rack. "We might be able to save him. This boy's not having that man's death on his conscience if we can help it."

Everybody pitched in and began dragging bones in a hurry. Roy brought a wheelbarrow. He and Hollis loaded smaller bones on it and rolled them off to one side and dumped them.

"Everybody be careful," Liam warned. "Don't want to trigger another bone slide."

With all of them working they soon found Wibb Orr's crumpled body. Blood seeped from the corner of his mouth. He looked lifeless to Hollis, but he hoped for his friend's sake that the man still lived, especially since he was to be sent away to the hospital.

The sheriff knelt beside Wibb Orr, feeling for a pulse and watching for the rise and fall of his chest. "He's alive, but barely," he said. "We'll have to load him in the back seat of my car—can't wait for an ambulance. Let's rig up a stretcher—rip off a shutter from the house."

Afterwards when they stood around the cars ready to leave, Liam said, "Roy, you come home with me. Go get your things."

"I don't have any things," Roy said.

Hollis and Roy squeezed in the back seat of Preacher Henry's car with Mr. Mayhew. Big Liam sat in front with the preacher.

"Call the hospital and let them know I'm coming," the sheriff said before starting slowly up the hill ahead of them with his load. The others took time to close the skull gate, then proceeded to Preacher

122

Henry's to make the telephone call. On the way they dropped Hollis off at Grancy's.

Lou and Grancy asked him no questions. They must have known he was so tired, in his mind and in his body, that he could not sit up. In fact, he fell asleep over supper. Lou helped him to his featherbed and didn't fuss a bit because he left most of his food uneaten.

22

HOLLIS LINGERED at the mailbox. He had brought water for Fannie-Dove's vine and was hoping the postman would come while he was there. Mom should be sending the return bus tickets any day. Hollis no longer feared that his parents might not take him back, but he needed to hold the tickets in his hands.

He squinted his eyes to look along the road toward the church and the covered bridge, expecting to see the nose of the mailman's pickup coming around the curve. The sun shone clear and bright, but Hollis noticed how far down the southern sky it had moved its east-west pathway—another sign that summer's end was near.

No pickup rounded the curve, but something else came lumbering into view—a big box with legs and a feathered hat. Hollis stared. He held onto the mailbox to steady his vision. The apparition came closer and closer. It still looked like a big walking box. Now Hollis could see a face with a lipsticked mouth—a woman hardly taller than himself but wide as a gate, carrying a suitcase and an umbrella. She stopped in front of him, set down her bag, and looked him over from top to bottom and back again. He was too dumbstruck to squirm.

"Let go of that mailbox," she ordered, "before you tear up my pet vine."

Fannie-Dove! She had come home.

Hollis unloosed his hold. She shoved the bag into his hand and turned to march toward the house. Her dress sported large red flowers. Her sandals exposed dusty feet with—Hollis counted them—six toes hanging out between the straps. The hand that clasped the umbrella like a drum major's baton had six fingers.

The dogs gathered in a quiet group inside the gate, eying Fannie-Dove cautiously.

"Well, mongrels," she said. "I see you're all still here."

Up the steps, across the porch, and into Grancy's room she strode. Hollis arrived with her suit-case—loaded with bricks it must be—in time to see Lou leap up, hastily closing the book she'd been read-ing to Grancy. Grancy's bed tray sat across her lap. Her plate held her favorite snack, a half-eaten popover oozing butter and honey. Her fork stopped halfway to her mouth.

"Who is it, Emmy Lou?" she asked.

"Well, well, Miz Orr," Fannie-Dove crowed. "What's the meaning of this? Why are you in bed? Did you break a leg?"

"Fannie-Dove!" gasped Grancy. "We wrote you to let us know when you'd be back."

"I can see why Your Majesty wanted to be warned. Lounging abed near noontime. With two lazy cats asleep on the pillow. A grown girl reading to you, and a half-grown boy at the mailbox tearing down my flowering vine. I should have come back sooner."

"Grancy's not well," Lou protested. "She's got her summer malady."

"We've been taking care of her," Hollis said indig-nantly.

"Not well?" Fannie-Dove snorted like Burdock. "She's never been sick a day since I've known her, and that's near 'bout a hundred years. Take my bag to my room, then let's get some order in this place."

She hung her feathered hat on a peg in the hall, tied an apron over her square body, and astonishing things began to happen. First, she took a broom and swept. Everything, including Samantha and Thompkins, flew before the relentless sweeps of Fannie-Dove's broom. "Cat hair, dog fur, spider webs, and lint," she chanted. "Sand and gravel, sticks and rocks. Look under this bed. Crumbs and peanuts. What did you people do while I was gone?"

She sent Hollis scurrying for mops and pails of water. She set Lou to scrubbing the kitchen floor and both of them to wiping up dust and washing windows. Fannie-Dove wouldn't believe how hard Hollis and Lou had worked while she was gone.

"And no more hoity-toity popovers," Fannie-Dove said, snatching Grancy's tray and shoving it at Hollis. "Peas and spinach and potatoes, Miz Orr. That's what you need. And as soon as the floor dries you get up out of that bed. No more waiting on you, my girl."

Fannie-Dove chose a dress out of Grancy's closet. "You got to stir around or you'll be helpless in no time, Miz Orr. You know that." She wagged her big square head and clicked her tongue. "What a sporty time you folks must have had. Popovers! Dogs and cats on the bed! A dog's a dog, I say, and a cat's a cat. If they don't do a dog's work or a cat's, they don't eat." Fannie-Dove banged and knocked and clattered, and the dust roiled.

23

THE CHANGE IN GRANCY astonished Hollis. She became meek, never disputing anything Fannie-Dove said, no matter what. He noticed, too, that the dogs kept a safe distance from Fannie-Dove. They didn't dare come on the porch to look inside.

"I just know my fine palm tree's as dead as a doornail," she proclaimed, tramping down the hall to the plunder room. "While you people frolicked the summer away, you forgot all about it." Her jaw dropped in surprise when she saw how green and flourishing it was in the redwood box by the window. She quickly recovered. "Well, it doesn't look too sick. But where'd all these crumbs come from? Crackers, cookies! Mercy on me! A sure way to bring a houseful of mice and ants in here. Away with this stuff!"

Checking her peanut patch from the plunder-room window, she seemed almost disappointed that it hadn't been smothered by kudzu. "What about my tools? Did you scrape every grain of dirt off the blades before you stored them? Did you make sure they're dry and won't rust? And the wheelbarrow has to be washed out. Make sure the shed door doesn't flap in the wind."

By the time Hollis took care of all that and returned to the house, a stranger sat in Grancy's chair.

She wore a blue dress with a lace collar pinned by a cameo brooch. She wore shoes and stockings. Her white braid circled her head like a crown. Hollis blinked. Grancy! Fannie-Dove acted as if she had created Grancy and Grancy belonged to her. "Here's the real Emmy Lou Orr," she announced. "She can peel the spuds for supper."

"But Grancy can't see," Lou protested.

"She can still peel potatoes. And shell peas. Just you wait till time to harvest the peanuts. She'll have her overalls on and be down in that patch pulling up plants right alongside me."

"Yes," said Grancy. "Come here, Emmy Lou and Hollis." She encircled each one with an arm. Hollis stiffly resisted, resenting how she had fooled them. But Grancy said softly, "I have been kind of in disguise this summer. I hope you won't hold it against me."

"You tricked us," Hollis said. Now he understood the signal that passed between Grancy and Josie that day. They were talking to each other without words.

Grancy said earnestly, "When your parents asked if they could send you here and told me why they were sending you, I knew I had to do something drastic to help. One thing I've always believed in: when you've got trouble, keep busy. I asked myself, 'How can I keep those two busy?'"

"So she had a brain storm," Fannie-Dove interrupted. "Get rid of me! Get old Fannie-Dove out of the way and take to her bed." She popped the dusting rag she was using to polish the mantel.

"I thought you might like being in charge, under my command of course." Grancy smiled. "You can guess that I'm not allowed to do much commanding any other time."

Fannie-Dove snorted. "I'd fear to see this place if you were in charge."

Grancy drew Hollis closer to her while she held Lou's hand. "I love you both very much. I hope you'll forgive me. I enjoyed every minute with you. You gave me the best vacation! The only one I ever had. Thank you."

Hollis relaxed against Grancy. "I had fun too. And I remember how I felt when we first came — like I was all in little ragged pieces, like I could never be whole again."

"That's exactly the way you seemed to me. I never saw a boy so all to pieces. But you're not now, are you? You're all right now." Grancy said that last very firmly, daring anybody to disagree.

"Yes," said Hollis, and he knew it was true. Whatever his parents worked out, they would still be his parents. They would always love him no matter what.

"Enough, enough," said Fannie-Dove, popping the dust rag again. "To the kitchen, everybody."

Hollis had to admit it was fun making supper ready. Fannie-Dove had cleared the table of cat bowls. "Cats belong on the floor," she said. She set her plants on the windowsill and spread a clean tablecloth. Now Grancy and Hollis sat at the table shelling peas and peeling potatoes. Lou mixed meatloaf, and Fannie-Dove made bread.

Before she began cooking, however, Fannie-Dove brought to the kitchen the low bench Hollis had sat on when he waited for the songful mouse. She placed it near the stove and stepped up on it. The bench raised her high enough to work well at the stove. When she needed to work at the counter, she pushed the bench there with her six-toed foot. "Mr. Will Orr made this for me," she said. "What a blessing it turned out to be. I couldn't reach a thing. That Josie girl was a big help too. How we miss her!"

"Maybe now she'll come back to stay," Lou suggested.

Fannie-Dove smiled for the first time. "Maybe she will at that."

By this time, Fannie-Dove had heard what happened in Bonepile Hollow. All she had to say was, "Served that Mr. Wibb right. He was the meanest man that ever walked on two legs."

Fannie-Dove even took charge of the reburial of Mr. Mims. No other bones besides the ones on the black board could be found. Hollis, Rufe, and Roy, with Liam's help, built a box big enough to contain the skull and the two bones. On a morning when the sky arched bright blue over the woods and the fall leaves shone red and yellow, they carried the box back of the cemetery, followed by everybody else, including Grancy and the dogs. With so many willing shovelers, Mr. Mims' grave was soon refilled and tamped down.

"May he rest in peace," Preacher Henry said, leaning on his shovel.

"Amen," everybody agreed.

"Next time we clean the cemetery," Liam said, "we'll take care of this plot too. It won't be forgotten again."

24

GRANCY WALKED around everywhere. She brushed her own hair and braided it. She dressed herself and made her bed and washed dishes. Hollis couldn't believe all the things Grancy could do without seeing. Now that she was out of bed and doing for herself, Lou and Hollis had more time to pack for the trip home. The only trouble was that interesting things kept distracting Hollis and binding him closer to Dolliver.

For one thing, he woke early on a day when a delicious fragrance blew in his window. He put his head outside and smelled in all directions—the delicious odor was everywhere. It was not a cooking odor, nor a perfume odor, nor a flower fragrance. "It's like I'm breathing purple grape juice," he explained to Grancy.

How she laughed. "You won't believe it," she said, "but it's your old enemy, kudzu. It's come into full bloom, and it smells so wonderful you feel like drowning yourself in the air."

Hollis couldn't believe her. The kudzu looked just the same, all thick green leaves. He ran below the peanut patch where the vines snaked out of the Hollow. After some intent searching, he found the beautiful clustered flowers, shades of purple and lavender, hiding under the large leaves. There were so many of them their fragrance saturated the air. He wished he could take some of it home with him in a bottle. Why not try? He washed a plastic bottle clean, set it in the sun to dry, then let the warm south breeze fill it with kudzu odor. He pictured himself at home surrounded by Mom, Dad, and Lou, opening the bottle to let them whiff the delicious Dolliver air.

He worried about what would happen after he left Dolliver. Who would keep the fast-growing vines from covering Grancy's house? He knew well what it would be like to return next summer and find only silent green mounds where Grancy's house now stood. Grancy reassured him.

"Kudzu rests in winter," she said. "It won't grow an inch while you're away. But it will be raring to go as soon as summer comes again. So you'd better hurry back."

Considering everything, Hollis felt better about the voracious green vine. He felt better toward Wibb Orr too. Grancy helped him understand that the man's most tragic mistake was in hating. "Hate rots the heart, Will used to say. And it's true. Wibb fed his heart on hateful thoughts. And it twisted his life."

Hollis remembered what Grancy said on the afternoon Rufe and Roy came over. The jealous twinges in his chest reminded him as Rufe, showing all his teeth in a grin, said, "Sheriff says Roy can live with us till they find his kinfolks."

"Never had no kinfolks," Roy added. "Don't remember any." He was grinning too, the first time Hollis had seen him look happy.

"Next summer, won't we have the dandy times?" Rufe said.

"Yeah," Hollis agreed. "Did you know that we're giving all the bones to any museums that want them? Maybe they'll rebuild a zeuglodon. Grancy says we could help them."

"Wow!" said Rufe.

Roy's eyes sparkled. Hollis knew how shy he must feel trying to handle all the changes in his life. He knew things could only get better and better for Roy, and he was glad. After that he felt no more jealousy, because he realized he had helped put that shine in Roy's eyes and the smile on his face.

While the boys explored the plunder room, looking at all the old things, Roy confided to them how he had sometimes slipped away from Bonepile Hollow to watch what other people were doing in Dolliver. He could never stay long for fear Mr. Wibb would catch him.

"He'd beat me for slipping off," he said. "Mr. Wibb could beat hard."

Hollis shuddered, remembering.

"How come you never told us? We would have helped you," Rufe said.

"Too scared," said Roy. "You might be like Mr. Wibb too."

"Now you know we aren't, don't you?" Hollis said.

Roy's happy grin as he looked from Rufe to Hollis was his answer.

A letter came from Mom, enclosing their bus tickets. Mr. Mayhew agreed to take them to meet the bus on a Tuesday morning. "Y'see," he explained, "the

134

bus comes FROM your town every Monday, Wednesday, Friday. Then it goes TO your town every Tuesday, Thursday, Sat'day. That is, less'n it gets a puncture or busts its carburetor. Then it might be off schedule."

"I hope it breaks down," Rufe said. "That way you can stay longer."

"They got to go," Fannie-Dove said. "Might as well get it over with."

Now that Hollis knew Fannie-Dove better, he understood that she wasn't as gruff as she sounded. Then too Grancy had talked to him one day when the two of them were swinging on the porch.

"Don't take Fannie-Dove too hard," Grancy said. "She's a little hurt because I sent her away for the summer. And she's more than a little mad because we could get along without her. She was counting on everything going to wrack-and-ruin because she wasn't here bossing. But instead, we had a real larky time. Her palm tree didn't die; her peanut patch wasn't covered over. And you cleared up terrible Bonepile Hollow, which none of us could do. She'll soon be feeling better."

Another time, Hollis told Grancy about the singing mouse and read some of his journal to her. "That's like an enchantment," she said with a look of wonder on her face.

Hollis decided to give his comic books to Rufe and Roy. He packed the panpipe and his journals in a hand satchel Grancy gave him. Also into the satchel he put a spearhead chipped out of dull red chert. Rufe said he and his pa had found it on the old Indian trail that followed Dolliver Creek.

Roy gave him a cloth bag, closed at the top by a drawstring and filled with zeuglodon teeth. "Big teeth like these are in the Hollow," he said. "Bucketsful of them."

Roy's gift went into the satchel, along with the bottled kudzu air. Hollis planned to carry them on-board with him so he could be sure they didn't get lost.

Grancy hefted the satchel and felt the thickness of his journal through the cloth cover. "For a boy who came here hating reading, writing, and arithmetic, I'd say you did very well."

Hollis could barely remember how much he hated school when he came to Dolliver. Now he thought it might be fun when school began. He could find out what his friends had been doing and tell them about his summer in Dolliver. That's what he'd decided to name his journal: "My Summer in Dolliver."

In Lou's hand luggage, along with her shuttle and all the lace she had tatted, was a big lunch made by Grancy and Fannie-Dove. Hollis knew how tasty it would be far down the road.

"We put in some extra," said Grancy, "so if there's somebody on the bus without a lunch, you can share yours."

Mr. Mayhew tooted his horn outside the gate. Roy, Rufe, Mrs. Mayhew, Grancy, and Fannie-Dove, accompanied by the dogs, helped them pile the bag-gage in the back of the pickup. Thompkins and Samantha watched from the porch. When Hollis hugged Grancy one last time, he said in her ear, "I WILL make a speech at your funeral. But don't die anytime soon, promise?" Grancy laughed and promised.

Fannie-Dove shook hands. Hollis didn't feel the least bit squeamish when those six fingers curled around his hand. But he did stare, because Fannie-Dove had claimed that she was descended from a queen of England named Anne Boleyn who also had more fingers and toes than was absolutely necessary. That sixth finger sprouted out of Fannie-Dove's hand beside her other fingers, and it looked just like the rest of them. Now she leaned toward him and whispered, "Having six of 'em helps me fight kudzu faster." Hollis laughed and so did she. Just as Hollis stepped up into the truck cab, he surprised Rufe by slapping him on the arm. "Touched you last!" he shouted, leaping into his seat, pulling Lou in behind him for a shield.

Rufe, after recovering from his first shock, went wild, dodging around trying to reach his arm through the window past Lou, to tag Hollis. Just as Mr. Mayhew revved the motor to roar off, Rufe succeeded in reaching Hollis. "Gotcha last," he yelled and whooped.

At that moment the postman pulled in to the mailbox. "We'd better see if there's mail for us," Lou said. While she got out to check, Hollis slipped from the cab and crept around the back end piled high with their luggage. Rufe, watching Lou and the postman, didn't see Hollis till he leaped out, smacking him and shouting, "Touched you last!"

Safely in the truck again, wedged low between Mr. Mayhew and Lou, Hollis escaped Rufe's frantic reaching. As the truck roared toward Preacher Henry's, Hollis watched Rufe and Roy in the side-view mirror chasing after them and eating their dust.

Preacher Henry was getting his mail out of the box. Mr. Mayhew paused for them to shout good-bye to him. It was only a moment, but it was long enough for Rufe to catch up, reach in, and tag Hollis with a shriek, "Gotcha last."

"Next summer," Hollis shouted back to Rufe and Roy. "I'll get you next summer!"

Then the old pickup rolled onto the wood floor of the covered bridge. Its cool shadow enfolded them. Hollis stretched to see the splashing water one more time, and glanced backward where his friends were leaping around Preacher Henry and waving. Hollis held tight to his satchel.

"Good-bye, Dolliver," he shouted across Lou and out the window. "I'll be back!"

ABOUT THE AUTHOR

Aileen Kilgore Henderson lives in Cottondale, Alabama, a place much like the one Hollis was sent to that mysterious summer—monster fossil bones, arrowheads along the creek bank, acres of kudzu, and, once upon a time, a covered bridge. She taught school in Northport, Alabama, Big Bend National Park, Texas, and Stillwater, Minnesota. Her volunteer work in art and history museums, scouting, education groups, and a shelter for homeless and abused women and children gives her a varied background of experience. She is married to a naturalist. Their daughter and her husband live in the rain forest of Costa Rica. Aileen Kilgore Henderson's stories have appeared in *The Children's Digest*, *Nature Friend*, and *Odyssey*.

If you enjoyed this book, you will also want to read these other Milkweed novels:

*Gildaen, The Heroic Adventures
of a Most Unusual Rabbit*
by Emilie Buchwald
Chicago Tribune Book Festival Award,
Best Book for Ages 9-12

Gildaen is befriended by a mysterious being who has lost his memory but not the ability to change shape at will. Together they accept the perilous task of thwarting the evil sorcerer, Grimald, in this tale of magic, villainy, and heroism.

I Am Lavina Cumming
by Susan Lowell
Mountains & Plains Booksellers Association Award

In 1905, ten-year-old Lavina is sent from her home on the Bosque Ranch in Arizona Territory to live with her aunt in the city of Santa Cruz, California. Armed with the Cumming family motto, "Courage," Lavina deals with a new school, homesickness, a very spoiled cousin, an earthquake, and a big decision about her future.

The Secret of the Ruby Ring
by Yvonne MacGrory
Winner of Ireland's Bisto "Book of the Year" Award

Lucy gets a very special birthday present, a star ruby ring, from her grandmother and finds herself transported to Langley Castle in the Ireland of 1885. At first, she is intrigued by castle life, in which she is the lowliest servant, until she loses the ruby ring and her only way home.

A Bride for Anna's Papa
by Isabel R. Marvin
Milkweed Prize for Children's Literature

Life on Minnesota's iron range in 1907 is not easy for thirteen-year-old Anna Kallio. Her mother's death has left Anna to take care of the house, her young brother, and her father, a blacksmith in the dangerous iron mines. So she and her brother plot to find their father a new wife, even attempting to arrange a match with one of the "mail order" brides arriving from Finland.

Minnie
by Annie M.G. Schmidt
Winner of the Netherlands' Silver Pencil Prize
as One of the Best Books of the Year

Miss Minnie is a cat. Or rather, she *was* a cat. She is now a human, and she's not at all happy to be one. As Minnie tries to find and reverse the cause of her transformation, she brings her reporter friend, Mr. Tibbs, news from the cats' gossip hotline – including revealing information that one of the town's most prominent citizens is not the animal lover he appears to be.

MISSION STATEMENT

Milkweed Editions publishes with the intention of making a humane impact on society, in the belief that literature is a transformative art uniquely able to convey the essential experiences of the human heart and spirit.

To that end, Milkweed Editions publishes distinctive voices of literary merit in handsomely designed, visually dynamic books, exploring the ethical, cultural, and esthetic issues that free societies need continually to address. Milkweed Editions is a not-for-profit press.